MW01234571

THE BRIDE OF CHRIST
A Love Story

ELIZABETH WOLFE

DEDICATION

To my Husband, Pat, who has always given me all the space I needed to be who I am called to be. His unwavering patience with all of my blunderings is invaluable as I **still** try to become who I am meant to be.

His efforts to help me in this latest project by cooking meals, washing dishes, answering and fielding phone messages, refusing to voice his fears concerning my traveling alone, always being here for me when I return and doing it all without complaining , are more than amazing. God bless you, Honey.

ACKNOWLEDGEMENTS

*T*here is no way to appropriately thank my dear friend, Sandra Snell, who while at times welcomed me as a guest in her home and at other times drove the 3 hour trip to my home; where she faithfully read, proofed, and edited the many versions of the text. Her suggestions and corrections led to great improvements for the finished work. Without her encouragement and dedication to seeing it finished; I might have long since given up. She is such a Godsend for me.

Others, whose invaluable help with my vast lack of computer savvy are our nephew Glynn, daughter Barbara, grandson Benjamin and friend, Tim. Without them, this manuscript would have never gone to print.

I also want to thank Shirley Friedman, Mary Kicklighter, and the WPU ladies who encouraged me by saying; "There is a book in you and we want to read it."

Most of all, I want to thank the Lord, who was the constant, faithful source of the wording and thoughts found here.

TABLE OF CONTENTS

INTRODUCTION

To say this began as a short talk some 6 years ago would only be a partial truth. Like most things, it began in the mind of God eons ago and has just made it onto some sheets of paper and onto the devices of this generation's writers and readers.

It is in the form of a novel. This is for two reasons: 1. that is how I believe I heard it as I began to write, and 2. most people will probably read a lesson in novel-form more readily than they would read a theological text. In other words, the book is like a spiritual "spoonful of sugar."

The book's main characters are allegorical as follows: Deborah, the Bride, represents our lost soul that is being lovingly restored by J.C., who represents Jesus—the Bridegroom/Lover of our souls. H.S. is The Holy Spirit/Interior Designer of our souls and Susan is indicative of any friend who keeps on presenting the news of Jesus until we decide to "just meet" Him.

For some readers, the use of J.C. in reference to Jesus may seem a travesty. However, for the sake of obedience to what I was hearing and also to the flow of the dialog, I chose to do so.

I too, had reservations when I first heard it that way. At least I did until I came to understand that when Jesus asked his followers, "Who do you (my chosen ones) say that I am?" Peter, for the ages past and for all to come, summed it up. He said, "You are the Christ, the Son of the Living God."[1]

So, whether we refer to Jesus as Wonderful Counselor, Mighty God, Prince of Peace, Everlasting Father, The Lion of Judah, or J.C., His true identity is forever settled. HE IS THE CHRIST, THE SON OF THE LIVING GOD!

Nothing changes who He is. Our souls' thinking and behavior does not move Him from His Love-Path, nor does Holy Spirit change by being referred to as H.S., the Interior Designer of the Bride of Christ's restoration projects.

Truly, as Romans 2:4 says; "It is the Goodness and Kindness of God that leads men to repentance (a change of mind and inner man to accept God's will)."

Hopefully, as you read their story with an open mind and heart, the characters will restore, replenish, and renew your hope in His steadfast Love and Goodness so that you can trust H.S. with YOUR "restoration project."

DEBORAH

"*I*'m getting married in the morning."
Deborah's heart sang as she scurried about with last minute preparations for the upcoming nuptials. "This is finally happening," she thought. "It seems as if we have been engaged for a long time."

Sitting, quietly sipping a cup of tea, she began to reflect on her life. Childhood had been a rather chaotic time. Not much nurturing, coupled with excessive and harsh discipline, all of which led to her becoming a rather wild, rebellious, young person. College was a whirl of parties, dates, and just enough study to present a good score to her parents; whose deaths a short time apart left her entirely on her own. Her job skills allowed her to live comfortably though not extravagantly, and because she was very personable, she kept a busy social calendar—the consummate party girl!!

Deborah smiled as she remembered meeting J.C. Susan, her best friend, insisted time after time that he was the one Deborah needed to meet—that she would adore him and he would love her. Deborah would laugh and reply; "I have all the lovers I need, thank you."

Then there finally was the day she agreed to meet him. Laughing, she remembered thinking, "He's the farthest thing from what I want. He's definitely NOT for me!" J. C., however, seemed oblivious to her opinions or her attempts to avoid him. He was always available when her friend Susan, who introduced them, arranged a meeting. Actually, **available** is an understatement. He was GLAD to be present where she was. It was as if he was "all about HER"!! In retrospect, it seemed he would just appear for no special reason, at the most unexpected times. There he would be, attentively, quietly leading her through situations that were uncomfortable or hurtful or joyous—anything, everywhere—it was amazing. [2]

J.C. was so different from the other men she had known. So different, in fact, that she could not believe anyone could be so genuinely caring and concerned. In which case, *genuinely* was the operative word. In the past, she had known a lot of "bait and switch" and was not in the mood for any more of that.[3]

For the longest time, Deborah held J.C. at arm's length, watching to see when he would show the angry side; the "my way or the highway" side. To her surprise, she could not find any circumstance that caused a change in his nature.[4] It seemed as though meeting her needs at the moment was his only purpose.[5] Susan kept saying, "Deborah, just get to **know** him,[6] you will **love** him; and I promise you he will never disappoint you."

Deborah wanted so much to believe this, but her first reference for men—and the one she could not seem to shake— was her father. His reactions to everything were totally negative and unpredictable. She was always afraid that something she said or did would set him off into a rage ending in her being beaten or accused with no explanation heard, believed, or good enough. Then, there were her brothers; who tormented her and treated her with disrespect and contempt.

Her thoughts turned back to J.C. He seemed so opposite in every way from her past experiences. No matter how she tried his patience, it never broke. No matter how she messed up in situations, he was never angry, nor seemingly, even surprised!! As a matter of fact, he used her errors to bring her to an understanding of WHY she behaved as she did and how she could turn it around for her good. In all, there was never condemnation or accusation.[7]

Deborah thought, "I don't remember exactly when I heard his proposal or even when I said yes, but I do remember how he wooed me with such patience, seemingly in amusement and joy until.......one day, it just happened."[8] "How fortunate, that J.C. asked me to marry him. He chose **me**, a total misfit!!!" She found herself sitting at the table grinning at the thought of this. Deborah now remembered the book J. C. had given her. He said it was written to teach her to reign in life as his bride. She also remembered Susan's telling her that J.C.'s father was a rich and powerful man with a royal bloodline. "Hmmm, never met him, but I will meet him tomorrow. I'll also get to meet J. C.'s identical twin, H.S." These thoughts were all so exciting!! How in the world would she ever be a fitting wife for someone with a kingdom—a royal background?? "Oh well," she thought, "he asked me; I accepted, and he will just have to teach me to live royally!!"[9]

As the day wore on, Deborah's thoughts were consumed by J. C. It seemed he was in everything she did…at least until she dropped the dish of pins she was holding, and they scattered everywhere. She frantically scrambled around picking them up, getting more perturbed by the minute. "DAMN," she blurted out. She felt so ashamed at her outburst. "What would J.C. think if he heard her say that?"

At that moment, she could see J.C. smiling at her with such patience—a gentle, kind expression that seemed to say volumes. It seemed to say, "Deborah, Honey, that is not who you REALLY are. You are NOT one who is anxious about a little dish of spilled pins. You are learning to REIGN in life's ups and downs. So you are above that slip from the position you now occupy. Just learn to BE who you now ARE!!"[10]

Again, the image of him that she saw and the words she heard were so real that it was startling. It was as if he was right there with her. In retrospect, it seemed he was ALWAYS right there with her. "Makes me feel all warm and fuzzy," she thought. As she laughed, it seemed he was laughing too. At this, Deborah quipped, "Well since you are here, help me pick up these pins!" again laughing even harder.

With this new perspective of her life, crawling around searching for pins suddenly became less of a chore and easier to accomplish. She found that the image of him as an ever present reality, laughing with her and accepting her gave her a new sense of freedom. She felt enabled to overcome all opposition to herself and her problems.[11]

Much later, with all her preparations done, Deborah tried to sleep. This proved to be futile as her mind wandered to the future. "Tomorrow… what will it be?? He said no rehearsal, that everyone knew their part. Then where will the dinner be? He said the table was already prepared.[12] Where will we live?" These thoughts went on and on, until finally; she drifted into a troubled sleep.[13]

THE DREAM

As she slept, Deborah dreamed she was at a fine restaurant. There were efficient, pleasant servers for each table. People were ordering, and delicious food was being brought to them. Deborah looked at her menu, and momentarily placed her order for a rare lamb chop and a salad with oil and vinegar dressing.

While she sat waiting for her meal, she noticed a strange phenomenon. The people at other tables were unable to eat the delicious food at their places because their arms were too long to eat from the plate in front of them. Instead, they were reaching out into the distance as if perhaps their sustenance was at a table out someplace beyond their reach; a table that did not presently exist.

Strangely enough, she also saw that because of their reaching into the future somewhere, they never even saw the food in front of them. They just gazed and stretched their arms as if trying to eat from some table or plate beyond their current, available place for nourishment. Deborah wanted to shout, "No, No! Look at what is in front of you—right here, right now. You're reaching too far away! Just adjust your chair so you will fit the space where you are at present, and you will find your feast."[14]

At that moment in her dream, Deborah noticed that she too had food in front of her. Were her arms going to be too long to eat of her lamb?? She was so hungry and the aroma of the food on her plate just whetted her appetite for the meal she had been served. Suddenly overwhelmed by fear of the present moment, she never tried her arm lengths to see if they would pass the test of her own "now". Instead, she became so anxious that she thought, "I've got to get out of here!! But, I'm hungry...what if there is no food 'out there'....what is going to happen?"[15]

Awakening in a cold sweat, yet still "in the dream"; Deborah felt the panic created by looking beyond what was "on her plate" at the moment. She felt the cravings for the opportunity to be filled with the delicious lamb. She felt the fear and insecurity of judging **her** outcome by what she saw happening to others. [16]

"Breathe....Breathe," she thought. Then, "Hm—m—m, don't think breathing or tea will do this. It's going to take some strong coffee to wake me from THAT nightmare." After her coffee, Deborah found herself dancing around and singing, "Thank you J.C. for loving me. Thank you for choosing me!!" She heard J.C.'s voice in her heart saying, "Love is never love until it is returned, so thank YOU, my dear."

The voice was so plain that Deborah turned quickly expecting to see him standing there with the twinkle in his eyes that was always present when he was teasing her. Seeing no one, she tried to quiet her racing heart. "What a wonderful person he is," she thought.

It bothered Deborah that she did not know more about his family. He spoke often about his father with such respect, and in response to her question about his mother; he simply smiled and replied that she was a kind, gentle person, and understood that he was special. He also said she loved him and encouraged him in his gifts and calling.

Pushing those thoughts away, she said, "Got to get going now. No more daydreaming. Let me see, no packing necessary as there will be no honeymoon trip now. He has business to take care of for his dad, and has assured me we will have lots of places to go later." He had told her he had a special dinner planned just for the two of them after the ceremony. Her curiosity wildly contemplated this event. She chose her clothes carefully and laid out her dresses for the upcoming occasions.

"H—m—m—m....O.K, wedding dress ready, dinner dress ready, AND DEBORAH

READY—well, almost—YEA!!" Looking at the chosen items, Deborah questioned the WHITE wedding dress as "white" did not exactly represent her history- BEIGE, maybe, but certainly not white. However, J.C., who knew her lifestyle prior to their relationship, had said with an assuring smile, "Wear the white one." When she hesitated, he said, with a slight emphasis on 'white', "Yes, the <u>white</u> one."[17]As she thought about it, she said aloud, "Strange....but fine with me if you want to see me as 'snow white'." Once again, she heard the familiar chuckle.

THE CEREMONY

*D*eborah heard the doorbell and hurried to see who it was. She was secretly hoping that, in spite of the fact that he agreed to honor her request not to see him until the ceremony, he had broken his word. "Now isn't that a silly thought. J.C. would never break his word to me or, probably, to anyone else."[18]

When she opened the door, Susan was standing on the other side with a huge grin on her face. "Hi, girl," she said. "What are you doing in your P.J.'s? You're getting married this morning!" Deborah whirled around as she rhymed, "That's me; Mrs. J.C.!!" They both giggled at the rhyming of her words, and then began talking about how her hair should be fixed, what time she should put on her dress,

...ld sit in the car on the way to the
...re the wedding would take place,
and on and on. But, the more they talked, the
more anxious Deborah became.

Her thoughts began racing wildly. What if
this naturally curly hair decides to "do its own
thing", what if this linen dress gets all wrin-
kled on the car ride, what if I wait too long
to get dressed.... ? Susan snapped her fin-
gers in Deborah's face. "**Wake up, Girl! Wake
up!! You're the bride!! The wedding can't
take place until you get there, so just calm
down!!**"The words," wake up" suddenly triggered the memory of her dream and Deborah
said, "Guess my arm isn't long enough to eat
from that table, eh? I need to enjoy this moment
and let all of that evolve as it will."

The two of them enjoyed the remainder of
their time together, laughing as they reminisced,
until finally; it was time to dress the bride. Susan
busily helped fix Deborah's hair, pressed places
on her dress that did not look quite right, and
suggested things about makeup, jewelry, etc.

Deborah suddenly looked up at Susan and exclaimed, "Susan, when are you going to go and get dressed? It's already so late!"

Susan laughed, "Have it all in the car, Madam. Fixed my hair earlier this morning and now I just have to slip into my dress and shoes, fluff my hair and makeup, and we're off!" "Thank heaven for Susan and her steady, confident air. It helps calm these butterflies," thought Deborah. True to her word, in what seemed like seconds, Susan was dressed and beautiful. She then helped Deborah into her simple, yet elegant white linen dress that she and J.C. had chosen.

As she looked into the mirror, she recalled the day she and J.C. selected her dress. Having chosen an ivory one that she thought more accurately reflected her background; she showed him her choice. As if reading her unspoken thoughts, J. C. said, "Will you please just try on this one? To me, it perfectly says who you really are." Of course, as it always seemed, J. C.'s choice for her was correct in every detail. Even now, as she stared at her image, she could not recognize the woman she saw. Susan's voice broke into her thoughts. "O.K. Lady, you look gorgeous, so quit admiring yourself and let's be on our way."

The ride to the garden was very quiet as Deborah tried to fit herself into the image of the woman in the mirror wearing that white dress. "What if I am a big flop as the 'white dress woman'" she pondered. "What if I am a huge disappointment to him—he is so perfect in every way…?" Then she thought about his family—his Dad. "What if they don't like me?" By now, the tormentors had wracked her brain and her nerves until Deborah was nauseous. As they arrived at the site, Susan looked over at her and said, "Honey, what in the world is wrong? You're as white as a sheet!"

Deborah did not answer, but thought, "Yeah, I probably match this dress I'm wearing." Suddenly, she heard the familiar chuckle and the nausea subsided a bit. At that moment, she saw J. C. reaching for the handle of the car door. He was smiling at her as if she were the only person there, and even before he opened the door, she felt his love invade the space between them. In an instant she was out of the car and in his arms—no nausea there![19]

As if he had read her fearful thoughts on her way to him, J.C. began to whisper the answers to all the questions of her inadequacies. "You are beautiful. You are also everything I have ever known you to be. Even before you knew me, I knew you and loved you.[20] There is no way you can disappoint me." With a chuckle he said, "As a matter of fact, I probably know what you are going to do before you know." Every time Deborah heard that chuckle, it was the most liberating force. It freed her, as opposed to condemning her.

Her thoughts had momentarily strayed from his voice, and she realized he was saying something else to her. "I'm sorry, what did you say?" she asked. "I said that I have told Dad and H.S. all about you and they love you as much as I do," he replied. Deborah's reply to this was simply a quiet, "Really?"

They were approaching the gazebo where Dad and H.S. were waiting for them. She felt J.C.'s arm tighten around her waist a bit. The Love she felt in the presence of the three of them was so intense that she almost melted into her shoes. As if that weren't enough, a joy began to rise in her; a joy that Deborah had never experienced before. It was akin to the feeling she had when she heard J.C. chuckle, but was, in comparison, uproarious and unquenchable laughter—the kind of laughter one cannot stop no matter how hard one tries.

The intensity of the moment caused Deborah to feel weak and faint, yet joyous. Every hair on her body seemed to stand on end. She was shocked—even fearful at the newness of the life she felt surging through her being. "Lord have mercy," she thought, "If J.C. weren't holding me; I would be lying on the grass!" Realizing they were all laughing at her reaction, she began to laugh too. When she did, she was shocked at the depth of her laugh. It seemed to surge up from a place that had been locked up or hidden before.[21]

"If this were not all so strange," she thought, "it would be the best place I've ever known." By now, his Dad, H.S. and Susan were making their way to their appointed spots for the vows and she and J.C. were alone." We'll just walk in together," he said. "Isn't that a bit nontraditional?" she asked. J. C. laughed, "My Dear, you will find that almost **EVERYTHING** about life with me is fairly nontraditional."[22] The service that followed made "simple" the understatement of the century—or at least in Deborah's understanding of wedding vows.

Susan read from J.C.'s family book about the results of Love. She read that Love isn't selfish and resentful, rather, it believes the best of everyone in all situations.[23] Then, H.S. read a passage about how men in their family Love their wives enough to give up their own lives for them.[24] Dad then asked if they would receive each other in this way. They each said, "Yes", and it was a forever settled Love Covenant.

There was no ring exchange or any of the things that Deborah thought should have been part of a "real" ceremony, but just as J.C. had said, he was not much on tradition. By now, Deborah was beginning to learn to submit to his plan, and it would bring her the desires of her heart. It was becoming more and more evident that, when her heart's desire was HIM, the things of real importance always became a reality.[25]

After the ceremony, everyone visited and enjoyed the simple refreshments they had planned and then, at last, they were alone. J.C. looked at her with a twinkle in his eyes and asked, "Shall we dance?" "Silly goose," she answered twirling to face him, "we don't have any music." J.C. said softly, "Listen to your heart, or to mine, and you will hear it." And she did.........

SHOPPING WHIRL

"J.C., I am suddenly so tired." Deborah said. "Well, my Dear, we have been dancing for an hour or more, so that isn't too surprising. We had best go. You see, we have another trip to take before dinner," he replied.

Stunned, she looked at him and asked, "Another trip....where or, maybe I should ask what?'"

"It's a surprise," he replied. "You see, where we are going will energize you immediately."

"Please, tell me," she begged.

Laughing, he said, "Can't you just trust me with this? I can promise you are going to love it.'"

"I'll give you this chance, but if I don't love it, am I supposed to trust you ever again?"

Smiling, he said, "That is something I will have to leave to you. There will be a lot of times you will have the opportunity for that choice, Deb."

She loved the way he called her Deb –so much more intimate and less formal. "O.K.," she said, in a jokingly submissive tone, "I'm going to trust you—this time anyway."

"You won't regret THAT decision, my dear," he said as he gave her a hug.

They left the garden laughing, talking, and teasing each other, and it seemed they had barely left when they arrived at a part of the city that was totally unfamiliar to Deborah. Shops lined both sides of the street. Some were beautiful and some more quaint in appearance.

"How did you find this place?" she asked. "I have never known it existed. It looks like a real shopper's dream—come—true."

"Another decision you will have to make in a bit," he said.

"Quit being so secretive, J.C., and tell me what you are up to now, pleeease!!"

"Oh, we're going to buy your wardrobe," he said nonchalantly. Her insecurities clicked in and she all but shouted, "WARDROBE?! I don't understand. What's wrong with the clothes I have now?" "There will be times when, as my bride, you are going to need special clothing," he replied. "I want you to know how to dress for each occasion. We are simply doing some advance preparation in order to outfit you appropriately."

Deborah's mind was once again racing into the future as she tried to envision what kind of occasions he meant and where they would take place. J.C. took her arm and guided her into a very elegant establishment. It had the name FAITH written above the beautiful glass doors that, in the late afternoon's sun, sparkled like diamonds. Unlike the shopping places to which she was accustomed, she did not see any racks with dresses on them. "Where are the clothes?" she whispered nervously.

"The attendant will bring some things out and you may choose what you like," he said.

At almost the same time she said "Oh", the attendant appeared. She was a beautifully dressed lady who seemed to know J.C well— something that Deborah filed in her mind for later questioning. "Deborah, this is Hope. Hope, this is Deborah", J.C. said. "Hope, we would like to see some outfits for Deborah's selection, please." Unlike Deborah, who was getting more uneasy by the minute, J.C. seemed quite at ease in this setting. Without looking, he realized her anxiety and reached out and took her hand. Just the touch of his hand suddenly stilled all the trauma of the unexpected, and she decided this was going to be fun.[26]

J.C. seemed to always be enjoying whatever he was doing at the moment. "So why can't I just get into the same mode and enjoy things too?" she reasoned. Hope brought outfit after outfit. Deborah was so overwhelmed that she just could not choose. They were ALL so beautiful!! Suddenly, J.C. said, "This one is perfect for you, Honey. Try it on and see what you think, please." Deborah thought the little silk, cream colored, sleeveless sheath lacked luster, but tried it on anyway. When she looked in the mirror, she thought, "Well if this is all Faith and Hope have to offer, I think we'd best shop elsewhere."[27]

"What do you think?" he asked when she appeared in the dress.

Deborah was trying hard to think of an answer that would be suitable when J.C. said, "I don't think you love it, do you?" Before she could answer, he turned to Hope with a twinkle in his eye and said, "Well, since Faith **works** by love,[28] do you have anything back there that could possibly make it a bit more 'lovable' for her?" With a confident smile, she left and came back with a gorgeous little jacket in the same cream color silk that was embroidered all over with a green design. It was perfect. Deborah put it on and gave a happy smile to both J.C. and Hope.

"I have some complimentary pieces for this particular outfit. Would you like to see them?" the attendant asked. She then brought out a beautiful green, silk scarf that she said was an original by someone that J.C. obviously knew as he approved heartily. Deborah agreed that it was now an outfit she now felt good about owning and wearing whenever the occasion was right. J.C. thanked Hope and they left the store.

"Thank you J. C. I'll always feel secure when I need to wear this," she said. "As a matter of fact, I think I liked just about everything I was shown there. Don't you think most of the things we saw there would be appropriate for some of our occasions?"

"Oh, I think the clothes from Faith and Hope's selections are probably going to fit perfectly into many, many situations we will attend together. I'm glad you like them as much as I thought you would."

J. C. put his arm around her waist and started toward another store.

"O.K., it's time for some fun stuff. Are you ready?" he asked with a mischievous grin.

"What?" she asked, again looking up at him with unveiled adoration.

"We are about to get you into an outfit that will immediately destroy any sign of heaviness the minute you put it on."

"Heaviness?!" she exclaimed. Looking at her backside in the glass of the storefront they were passing, she said, "Do, you think I'm too heavy?"

He laughed as if this was totally absurd. "I think you are absolutely beautiful in every way, silly. What I mean is *thoughts* that are heavy with fear or depression—that sort of heaviness."[29]

About that time, they arrived at the store. They could hear the music that was coming from inside—LOUD MUSIC!! When they entered the huge store, there was so much noise everywhere. In one corner, there were people very quietly singing Blessed Assurance. In another, there were people with guitars, drums, trumpets, and violins singing at the top of their voices. In yet another, there were people visiting with each other and sharing stories of their triumphs and joy. IT WAS LOUD!! Deborah covered her ears and looked at J.C. who just laughed at her.

"What is the name of THIS PLACE?" she yelled.

"PRAISE," he responded in a loud voice.

"I don't like it in here," she said, equally as loud.

"A lot of people don't like it, but it is one of my **favorite** places, so please learn to be part of it and enjoy being in it," he said. J.C. laughed and made a slight motion toward one of the clerks who immediately went and brought out a dress that just made Deborah want to laugh. Now mind you, it wasn't ugly—just FUN!! It was made of hot pink sequins interspersed with the shiny, round, orange, metal bangles that she had seen sewn on purses, etc. When Deborah put it on, she whirled around and the **dress** made noise too!! Suddenly everybody started laughing at the noisy dress and they laughed for quite a while. The music changed, and soon everybody was dancing and singing together. Deborah, being something of a party girl, was all about it. J.C. looked at her and said, "My dear, Praise looks gorgeous on you." At this, they all laughed even more!![30]

When they left the Praise store, J.C. said, "There are a couple of other things we need to purchase to make your wardrobe ready, at least for a while." Still, in the mood of the last garment's purchase, Deborah smiled and said nothing—just happily followed along.

They arrived at the next store where the atmosphere changed from loud to a very soft, sweet Presence. Suddenly, as if supernaturally, J.C. draped a soft cloak over her shoulders. The touch of it along with his hands on her shoulders almost made Deborah melt into the plush carpet of the store. The whole moment made Deborah look up at him questioningly. He smiled and said, "You are at the Mercy Store."

Trying to take in the feel and the Presence she was sensing, Deborah lifted the edge of the cloak to look at it more carefully. "Surely there must be some magic in this wrap," she thought. "I've never felt anything so wonderfully soft and comfortable."[31] As she stared at the garment in her hand, she realized it somehow changed colors as she turned it in different directions. At this realization, she again gave J.C. a look of childish wonderment and whispered, "This is so different. I mean…." her voice trailed off.

"It will be new in the morning, J.C. told her."

Shocked, she said, "You mean a whole new color?"

"No, it will be completely new **every morning** an entirely new cloak of mercy for you to wear tomorrow."[32]

Trying to be a good, frugal wife, she said, "Oh Honey, this one is fine. I really like it a lot, and don't you think it is a bit foolish to have one for every day?"

"No, you see, your mercy needs may be different and greater tomorrow than your mercy needs for today. So, when you wake up, **immediately** start looking for and **expecting** mercy. You will see a whole new version of it tailored just for that day."

Once again, Deborah's finite mind could not take in what he was saying, so she just nodded and wrapped herself tighter in her cloak of mercy.

Down the street a bit was their next stop. The store had no fancy front entrance, like the places they visited earlier. There was very simple music playing in the background. Here there were actually racks with clothes hanging on them. Deborah noticed that the clothing here was strikingly different. However J. C., who was intently trying to choose the perfect garment from among them, seemed oblivious to this.

"This will be one of my favorite outfits for you," he said, casually pulling a very plain, cotton dress from a rack.

"Where would I ever wear *that* thing?" she asked condescendingly. "What is it?" she asked. "It looks like a housedress to me."

"The designer called it her 'Humility' line. Hasn't been **her** biggest hit either, but I love it. Hopefully you will learn to enjoy wearing it as much as I will enjoy seeing you do so," he said quietly.[33]

"We'll have to see about that," she said a bit curtly.

J.C. just smiled and replied, "We only have one more stop before dinner: how are you feeling now? It's been a long day."

Feeling a bit contrite at his concern, following her sharp retort, she smiled and said, "No, I'm fine. Let's go and see what you have for me": all the while thinking, "It can't be worse than this one." The grin on J.C's. face made Deborah a bit uneasy, and not without just cause. They walked and walked, and the surroundings became less and less glamorous. After what seemed to Deborah an eternity, he stopped at a very small, but neat, shop.

"I guess, seeing how large this place is, not many people know about it or shop here," she thought. "It is sort of hard to find." They went inside and the lady who appeared seemed very glad to see them. Deborah could not help but wonder if this was because they were the only customers she had seen that day!

"Could we see one of your dresses?" J.C. asked politely. With a smile, she nodded and disappeared. When she returned, she had in her hands a dress made from a sack,-a **BURLAP SACK!!!** Deborah looked at him in disbelief. "This has gone waaay too far," she thought. Thinking it must surely be a joke, she decided to play along. "And where will I be wearing this one?" she asked with a big grin.

"Why don't you try it on?" he said.

Not to be outdone, she agreed. Immediately, she regretted that decision. "Oops, sorry," she said flippantly, "it's too tight, and it is ever so scratchy; not to mention that it's not my color. Could you get your money back? I pretty much hate it."

"No, it can't be returned." Rather poignantly, he said, "You see, I bought it a long time ago to be part of your wardrobe."

Laughing at this, she said "How much could it have cost-surely not much? Let's just let them have whatever it cost and not get it, O.K.?" Deborah pled.

"Since you want to know what it cost, I will tell you. It cost me my life-all I had."

She started to laugh again, but when she looked at him; she opened her mouth to apologize instead. He raised his hand as if to silence her. "You see, Deborah, there were malicious and unrighteous witnesses who could not understand me so they became envious, rose up and accused me falsely.[34] I paid a very high price for their unwillingness to believe I meant them no harm. Instead of retaliating, I prayed for them when they were sick and ministered to them in their distress. It was all part of the plan for me. Now it is part of the plan for you as my bride. You will have many occasions to wear this garment and, yes, it will be very uncomfortable until you become accustomed to its fabric. Then you will wear it and be unaffected by it,—I promise. By the way, it looks beautiful on you."[35]

"Who in the world would design a dress like this?" she asked sincerely.

Laughing, he said, "Well, it was a rather unworldly person and this particular style is called 'Forgiveness'."[36]

"Tell me I don't have to wear it to dinner," she said with a little smirk.

"Not if you love and forgive me for buying it for you," he laughed.

Deborah put on her dinner clothes and trying not to show how happy she was to be free of that garment; she smiled sweetly at the clerk. Adding it to their purchases, they left for the promised dinner. Deborah realized she had hardly eaten anything all day and said, "I'm starved. What's for dinner?" "You'll just have to decide that when we get to the restaurant," he replied, smiling.

OFF TO DINNER

$\mathscr{A}$rriving at the restaurant for dinner, they were immediately seated at a table set with beautiful china, silver, and crystal. Deborah was still looking around in amazement at the beautiful appointments when the waiter arrived to get their drink orders and tell them about the special foods being offered that evening. He answered questions about the items on the menu that interested them. Then, he explained that some of their selections had been prepared for viewing prior to making final choices. "These," he said, "can be seen across the hall in a room designed for this purpose."

Since Deborah did not recognize some of the menu's items by their names, she asked J.C. if they could go and see the prepared food. As they walked across the room, people spoke to J.C. He always introduced Deborah and responded to their greetings with favor and kindness. Once again, Deborah was amazed at the man she had married. He seemed equally at ease in this elegant place as he had in that last little hovel of a store where they bought that awful burlap dress. Even now, she shivered at the thought of it.

"Are you o.k.," he asked?

"I'm fine," she replied. Then, in a flashback to how he always knew her thoughts and not wanting to start her marriage by hedging on the truth, she said, "I was just thinking about that last outfit. Br-r-r-r-!" she said. He laughed, and they continued their way across the dining room, speaking to people as they went. She was getting hungrier by the minute as she saw and smelled the food on plates at the tables they passed.

"Do you know everybody here?" she finally asked.

"I know some of them much better than others, but yes, I know them all," he responded. [37]

"You seem so concerned about how they are, their families, their jobs—everything about them," she said.

"That's my job, and I love it," J.C. said as he looked around the room smiling broadly!

"You are a P.R. Person, eh?" Deborah said as she gave him a little sideways glance and smiled.

"That is what I do for my Dad's company," he said. [38]

"How did I not know that?" she asked.

"Deb, honey, there are so many things you are going to be learning about me—probably forever."

"Well, why don't you just tell me about it, Mr. P .R?"

"I assume you mean Personal Relations and that is a huge part of my responsibility. However, I am also the 'Person Responsible' for the company's benefits.[39] I handle 'Profit Returns'[40] and 'Passage Rights'[41] come under my umbrella. So, yep, I guess you could call me Mr. P.R.," he said grinning down at her puzzled face.

By this time, they had reached the other dining room where there were two tables. Both tables had food prepared and set out to help the diners with their menu choices. The largest table was set with gorgeous serving pieces containing the most scrumptious looking food Deborah had ever seen. Across from it was another table set with more simple, but elegant serving pieces filled with food that was prepared well, but with less appeal to one's visual senses. J.C. made his way toward the more simply prepared and garnished food. Deborah followed along wondering, "Why in the world does he want to pass by all this delicious food? He doesn't even seem tempted to look at it!"

As they approached the second table, she noticed that, unlike the larger table; these dishes had little porcelain name plates beside each dish explaining what was in it. The names had words like, Courage, Strength, Perseverance, Excellence, and Morality included in their descriptions. Other plates had the same names as the clothing he had just given her, Faith, Praise, Mercy, Humility, and Forgiveness. When she asked about this, his gentle response was, "Being outwardly clothed correctly is one thing, but having this correctness **inside** becomes another whole part of our marriage process."[42] More confused than ever, Deborah just said, "Oh."

In the center of this table was a huge arrangement of fruit: large, luscious fruit. Actually, it was the only really luscious-looking thing on the table. She commented on the difference in the appearance of the fruit and the prepared dishes. "Your fruit is so important for you, Deb. We need 9 servings per day," he replied. [43]

By now, she was a bit bored with all this conversation that she did not understand and wanted to get on with their meal. Rather curtly she said, "Well, you just eat your fruit while I go over to the other table and decide which of those delectable creations I will have for dinner."

"Hope it doesn't make you sick, Honey," he said quietly.

By now, she recognized that quiet tone as a warning about whatever she was about to do. "Why doesn't he just yell STUPID, THAT IS WRONG," she thought. Having followed her he asked, "Did you notice there are no cards on the table with the names of the ingredients in these dishes?" he asked.

"I suppose YOU KNOW what is in all of it," Deborah said.

"Pretty much," he again replied quietly.

"That is fine, but I think I will just have the dish here in the silver casserole."

J.C. smiled as he said, "That is fine with me. We will tell the waiter."

"What are you going to have?" she asked.

He started over toward the other table and Deborah stopped him.

"What did I select?" she asked, "Is it something that is going to hurt me?"

With a chuckle, J.C. said, "It killed me, but I free you to have as much of it as you please. I will love you whatever you eat."

"What do you mean it **killed** you?" she asked in a startled tone.

"Deborah, I told you that malicious people who could not understand me as I really am, felt threatened by me and instead of trying to hear me; they plotted to kill me because I did not fit their image of Godliness. It was all such a mockery—and still is."

"O.K. then, I'll just have that casserole over there. Will that be alright?"

Again, he called her by her entire name— another thing she was learning was a signal to pay attention. "Deborah, you are free to choose anything on the entire menu. I did not marry you to put you into a cage. I married you to set you FREE. Free to choose whatever you wish.[44] I will even help you overcome the consequences of your choices and never condemn you.[45] So, you just feel free to choose your meal."[46]

"Alright, what's in it?" she asked in a disgusted tone.

"It is a mixture of anger, resentment, and bitterness. All of this is held together by a sauce called strife containing every evil thing.[47] It tastes so good and is real comfort food for those ignorant that its sentence is death, not only to them, but to all those around them."

"The reason it is so deadly, Deborah, is because it looks so good. The deception is that the more one eats, the more one believes their problems are the fault of everyone else. Hence, they can NEVER become the person they were MEANT to be, nor can they let others be who THEY really are."

As he said this, Deborah envisioned a photograph of her family beside that casserole, and she decided their strife went back many generations. It seemed a good idea that the time to stop eating of that particular dish was RIGHT NOW!!

As she stared at that imaginary photo, she could not see some of her family members. She liked to think that maybe they had eaten from

Grace, Mercy, and Truth to escape the tortures of that dish. "I hope so," she said aloud. J.C., of course, understood her remark and no other conversation was necessary. They chose to eat from the table that contained life and health to all their flesh. [48]

It had been prepared very tastily and each recipe had been in the test kitchen to see if it would satisfy the hunger of the clientele who would be wise and choose from its nourishing, life-giving ingredients—Love, Joy, Peace, Patience, Gentleness, Kindness, Faithfulness, Goodness, and Self- Control.

Deborah was to learn that in order to watch her diet she had to choose from dishes without a lot of unhealthy "fat" in them. As they ate the food, Deborah listened to the sound of his voice as he talked to her about their life together. It was as soothing as sitting beside a gently moving stream and hearing the sound of the water.

HIS GIFTS

*T*he next morning, as they sat on the veranda together, J.C. took her hand and said, "Now, I must tell you that you have yet to see the most valuable gifts that I have for you."

Deborah was ecstatic, expecting some huge boxes all beautifully gift wrapped. Where were they? Was the USPS going to bring them for her? Maybe they were in their room.............. Suddenly reading her thoughts, J.C. interrupted, "Not this time," he laughed.

"The first gift I have for you is my Name.[49] You see, my Name denotes my nature. You and I are now to become one because, As I AM, so are you in the world.[50] So, you must take on my nature and let my Spirit rule over your circumstances.[51] In order for my Name to bring you honor, and set you on High and protect you in trouble, save and deliver you; you must realize its meanings and take on the same characteristics."[52]

"I don't know about all of that," Deborah responded. "I've always pretty much been my own person."

"Yes, and that is one of the things about you that I have loved so much. You don't shrink back when you are challenged in who you are—or at least, in whom you have always believed yourself to be."[53]

Feeling who she believed herself to be was about to be challenged by J.C., Deborah hesitated and then said, "Are you inferring that who I believe myself to be is wrong?"

"No, No," J.C. said as he reached out and again reassuringly took her hand. "What I am saying is, who you have believed yourself to be is limited."

Once again thinking she was being insulted, Deborah became defensive. "So you have married someone who is not right for you, and you are going to start off by trying to change me into a carbon copy of yourself?"

"No....and yes, I am just going to give you some skills that you **already have** as my bride, but you have not been aware of them. So, you have not yet made them part of the beautiful person you already are," he answered calmly. [54]

"I'd rather have something in a tiny box with a bow on it—like a big diamond ring," she said, pretending to pout.

J.C. threw his head back and laughed uproariously. "That is what I love about you, Honey. There is no pretense in you. You just tell it like you see and feel it, and that works fine when it is just the two of us. However, in circumstances as my bride, you will need that tempered with some characteristics that do not come as easily for you."

Suddenly, Deborah remembered the events of yesterday—the shopping trip, the dinner and all those dishes, the picture of her family, and she began to understand what he was trying to tell her.

"Does all of this have anything to do with those clothes we bought at the stores that had those religious names and the dinner dishes that I was not supposed to eat?" she asked.

"If I say yes, how would that make you feel?" he asked.

"I guess I would just feel defeated already and wonder if I will ever be right for you or please you," Deborah said fearfully.[55]

"Rest assured, my dear, that I have known forever that you are exactly right for me and fit perfectly in the kingdom I have prepared for you," J.C. continued. "When you received my name, you received a lot of things to prepare you to operate both in and out from this kingdom. Actually, you received **everything** you will need."[56]

"Like what?" Deborah asked.

"Like my Name. You accepted me as your bridegroom thus accepting my family's name. When Dad gave me this name, he attached great benefits to it. Now, those benefits belong to you as well."[57]

"You mean like job perks?" she asked.

Laughing aloud at the comparison, he said, "Well, yes, sort of like that only much more beneficial and lasting."[58]

"Do I still have the benefits if you divorce me?" she asked in a very serious tone.

Still smiling at the thought of that, J.C. said, "Now why do you think I would do that?"

"Because I may never get all this kingdom—reigning and benefits—stuff right," she said.

"You have the pattern all wrong, Honey," he said gently. "My name is my NATURE. The more you seek to understand my Name/Nature and its benefits, the more you will know me. The more **you** know **me**, the more secure you will become in who **you** really are."[59]

"How long will all of this take? Will there be a test to see if I am renewed—or whatever?"

J.C. quietly explained, "**Everything** in life with me is a test. The good news is that you can't fail. You just get to take it again and again until your mind is free to understand who <u>I AM</u> <u>in you</u>. Then, you can **be** that."[60]

Deborah was thinking, "This is not exactly what I bargained for. I thought it was all going to be about me."

"Would you like to know about your other gifts?" he asked.

"If you don't mind, could we just go for a walk first? I'm a bit overwhelmed right now."

The street was filled with lovely homes which had neatly mowed, trimmed lawns and beautiful flowers. As they walked, the aromas were a heady mixture of jasmine, honeysuckle, and sweet shrub. They walked for a long time in silence. Neither of them seemed to mind that there was no conversation. They were each simply enjoying the other's presence.[61] After a long time, Deborah said, "This walking is making me hungry. Let's get some lunch." J.C. agreed. They found a small café and sat down under the umbrella of a sidewalk table. "Whew! I'm too out of shape for all that walking, but weren't the yards and the flowers beautiful?" she asked.

"Not more beautiful than you," he replied looking deeply into her eyes.

The meeting of their eyes in such a direct gaze, and the love she saw there was so overwhelming that Deborah felt suddenly weak. "He can see everything I am thinking and feeling, all the way down into my deepest heart," she thought.

"J.C., you always make me feel so special and adored. Yet you know I am not so adorable," she spoke rather breathlessly. Then, laughing she said, "See, you take my breath away!!"[62]

"I would like to believe that, but I tend to think it had more to do with all the walking," he said with a big grin.

As they were eating, Deborah said, "J.C., earlier I think I was a bit defensive and so afraid of failure as your bride that I just couldn't hear clearly what you were trying to say to me. Try me again, please. I don't know how I will react this time, but, hopefully, better than before. What I **do know** is that you only want what is good for me."[63]

J.C. smiled and said, "I've been thinking about it. All the gifts that I want for you are described in the handbook I gave you. You can learn about all of them from it. I just thought if I explained some of them, it might make all of it more easily grasped."[64]

"O.K., Professor, your pupil is all ears," she joked.

"Actually, there are so many gifts I have for you that you will spend eternity unwrapping and learning to use them."[65]

"Well right now, you only have about an hour before I am going to be napping, so shower me with gifts, please," she said holding her hands up as if to receive a deluge of gifts.

"Of all that I have for you, this gift is the most important. So I will tell you about this one now. What I have for you is a personal trainer. His name is Holy Spirit—you know him as H.S. He will train you to use the other gifts you will find as you study the handbook. He is such a marvelous teacher. He knows the truth about all the tests you will have and will give you the answers if you will learn to consult him and accept him as Reality. You see, Deborah, he knows who you are created to become in the kingdom, and will teach you how to receive. That is the key—RECEIVE. First, you have to be open to receive HIM. Once you have done that, he will show you how to receive the two gifts that will cause you to reign in life. He raised me up from a very desperate place in my journey and gave me my life back. He will do the same for you and anybody else who will let him. He LOVES his work. He's the most valuable gift I can give you. He is truly the 'gift that keeps on giving'."

"In other words, he will help me to learn my role in your kingdom?" she asked.

"As you learn from him you will walk in newness every day. It's miraculous how he fills you with his wisdom, and honor, and glory. It's like giving you myself."

"Well, when will he get here? Hopefully soon, as he certainly sounds like someone I am going to need badly. All of this is so new to me, and truthfully; I feel very inadequate right now."

"Inadequacy is one of his best subjects. He will be giving you tools to show you the way out of that trap and all the others."

"Really, like what?" she asked, now getting almost as excited about all of it as J.C. was.

"If I tell you everything, Holy Spirit might lose his job," he teased.

"Well, I'm greedy enough to want to know what the other gifts you mentioned are."

"I love your appetite to learn about the kingdom you will reign in as my bride. Two gifts are additional things that you will have to learn to RECEIVE. When you receive the gift of Grace, which is my constant favor for you, you will be empowered by grace to overcome everything that would keep you from being who you were created to be. That, along with the free gift of Righteousness, which is right standing with my Father, will cause you to reign in life with me."[66]

"When will Holy Spirit get here?" she asked again.

"When we invite him, he will come. He is a gentleman, so he will just wait to be asked to take over, to be received as the guiding force for your life. At that point, he starts his training program."

"He won't wake me up for at least an hour will he?" she teased.

"Didn't I say he was a gentleman? Let's go get that nap."

Deborah pondered all of this as she walked back from the restaurant. She was so excited to know she was going to have her own trainer for the road to reigning. Suddenly she stopped walking and turned to J.C., "Will I have a throne and crown and all that goes with reigning?" she asked.

J.C. just responded with a hug and the familiar chuckle.

HER HOUSE

On one of their frequent walks, J. C. said, "Let me show you a neighborhood I don't think you have seen before." "Sure," Deborah said. She was gradually learning to trust him and reap the rewards of doing so.

The neighborhood he chose was breathtakingly beautiful. Each of the huge houses was surrounded by spacious lawns that had been meticulously cared for. The landscaping had been carefully planned and the plantings were gorgeous. As Deborah peeked through the gates at the magnificent homes and gardens, she oohed and aahed at every one. At the end of the street, in a cul de sac, was a huge house with brilliant light coming through the large windows. The light was so brilliant that it seemed to draw her toward it.

"WOW," Deborah thought, "I wonder who lives there."

He seemed oblivious to her thoughts. So she said jokingly, "Is that where we will live?"

He smiled and said, "Not at first, but we will live there more and more as we grow more intimate in thought and purpose."

Clueless as to the meaning of this she asked, "So you have other houses than this?"

Laughing, he said, "Oh yes, lots of them."

Remembering the stores where everyone seemed to know and respect his authority, she asked, "Do they have names – like the stores where we went shopping?"

"Yes, all of them have names. One of them is named Deborah."

"Sure it is," she said, thinking he was once again teasing her. "Is it this one?"

"As a matter of fact, it is," he said.

Stunned, Deborah just stared at him in unbelief. After a long time searching his face to see if this was all just something he was teasing about, she began to try to take in all of it. Staring at the house and occasionally glancing at J.C.'s face, she finally began to believe him. This was HER HOUSE!

"Don't let me believe this if you are not being truthful with me, J.C."

At this, he turned her toward him and looked straight into her eyes. "Deborah, there is something you must know about me. I cannot be untruthful. I may tease you and laugh with you, but I will never deceive you in any way. What I say is what I mean. You are looking at your house."

"Oh, GLORY! Thank you J.C! I think we'll be so happy here, don't you?"

"I believe I will and hopefully you will be too," he said.

Once again, as she turned to look at the beauty of it, she suddenly realized how many rooms there must be that would have to be cleaned.

"J.C., will I have servants or will I have to clean this entire house alone? That could take a lifetime of work. If I have to clean it, I don't know that I want to live here."

"There is already a well trained staff to meet every need for your house. You will, of course have to learn how to direct and use each of their unique abilities. It will take time and practice, but each time you use them, you will see how their ability to do their jobs has increased in proportion to your understanding of their purposes and directives."

"So they just stay in the house all the time and are there whenever I need them?" she asked.

"No, actually, they are now your servants and they will go everywhere you go and will serve whatever your needs may be."

"Do you know their names?" she asked. "I guess that is something I need to know."

"You, too, are familiar with their names. Until now, you have had only a casual acquaintance with them, but you are going to learn their true identity as they help you in your house."

"Oh, this is sooo exciting," Deborah said. "When will I meet the servants? When will we move in? Please, J.C., let's live there soon."

For some time, Deborah stood looking at the magnificent house that J.C. had said was theirs. He loved the fact that her eyes were wide and misty with the thought of her beautiful home which he had paid for her to have. Saying nothing, he just quietly watched as she stared at it with hands clutched in front of her heart.

Finally, he said, "We have to get going. It's late and we will have all day tomorrow to meet the servants and speak with them about their job descriptions."

Wheeling around excitedly, she squealed, "TOMORROW? Does that mean we will live there soon?"

With the familiar chuckle that she loved, he looked at her and said, "In your heart, I believe we are already living there."

Understanding nothing of that remark, Deborah thought, "OK, whatever." Then she said, with a chuckle of her own, "You know, J.C.

sometimes you say things that make no sense—at least to me they don't."

Laughing, J.C. said, "Well, you just give me time and maybe I'll get better at that."

As they walked away, Deborah saw that little twinkle in his eyes and knew there was something more she was going to learn about this.[67]

THE SERVANTS

inally, morning arrived and Deborah practically choked down her breakfast in anticipation of the meeting.

Looking at J.C., she said, "I have read and heard that when meeting one's employees, one should keep a straight-faced attitude. Is that what I should do this morning?"

At this, J.C. laughed harder than Deborah had ever seen him laugh.

Perplexed by his reaction to what she thought was a perfectly viable question, she asked, "What is so funny?"

"You're trying to DO everything so perfectly, Deborah."

"Well, as your bride, I have certain respon-sibilities and a position to uphold. I will have to manage our house and the servants correctly, and they need to know up front who is in charge."

As much as J.C. wanted to laugh even harder at this revelation, he knew and loved her heart. So, instead, he said gently, "Honey, your servants know how to appropriately meet the needs of your house. They are career professionals in what they do. They are trained by one who has designed each for his position of ministry, and you can trust their faithfulness." Bewildered by all of this, Deborah sat quietly for a bit. J.C. did not interrupt her thoughts as he knew she was trying so hard to be whom she was called to be and just did not yet fully understand her position.

After a few silent moments, he said, "Deb, just learn about them and their jobs. In time, you will trust their judgment. They will help perfect every room, and you will love the work they do. Their work will teach you how to move in REAL authority—the kind that causes obedience from respect and peace, rather than out of fear."

"Well, let's go do it," she said with a bit less enthusiasm.

They walked to the house in silence. Deborah was still trying to decide how to appear to them, and J.C. was letting her work through all of it in the only way she now knew—PAINFULLY. He smiled inwardly and said nothing as he envisioned the REAL Deborah. Later, at the house, Deborah was surprised to see those who stood awaiting their arrival.

First, there was Grace. As she was introduced, Deborah smiled a greeting to Grace, and thought, "I hope she and I will be as close as J.C. pictures." Grace responded with a broad smile and nodded in response. At which moment, a tall, erect, handsome young man stepped up beside Grace.

J.C. said quickly, "Deborah, this is Righteousness. He works closely with Grace. You are concerned about your position here and they are trained to teach you how to reign in Life with me. Receive them in that capacity and your understanding of position will increase and cause you to know who you are destined to be."

"Grace will teach you how to receive provision for overcoming the things about your house that you do not like and want to change. She also will show you favor in instances when your circumstances seem overwhelming and you feel out of control. You are going to be very blessed by the efforts of both Grace and Righteousness. Learn their ways and use them to their best advantage."

Next to Grace, was a young lady with the most peaceful facial expression Deborah had ever seen. She did not appear to be anxious about her introduction, or about all the generous compliments paid the other two. She just quietly waited for her place in the house to be announced and described. Deborah thought, "She is so calm. I wonder if she will be a hard worker."

As if reading her thoughts, J. C. said, "Deborah, this is Serenity. She will help with making things in your house run smoothly. She will not be obtrusive and often you will need to find her in order to best take advantage of her amazing abilities to put a new face on things."

"Where will she be that I will need to find her? Won't she live in the house?" Deborah asked.

"Oh yes, she will always be in the house. She will at times, however, not be in the same part of your house that you are in at the moment. For instance, if you are in the dining room, she may be upstairs rearranging your bed so you can rest better at night. Or she may be in the kitchen telling the servants what to prepare for your meals so that you can better digest your food. When you are in critical situations, she is always present in the house with ways to bring peace, but you will, at times, simply need to find her. To answer your question, yes she is always present."

Two people approached. They were holding hands and looked very distinguished. J. C. looked at Deborah and said very seriously, "Deborah, you must get to know these two." Pointing to the lady, he said, "Meet Wisdom." Then to the man, "Meet Understanding. These are the principal people.[68] They work together to guard and protect your life while they exalt and bring honor to you."[69]

Shocked, Deborah whispered, "Protect!? Guard my Life!? J.C., am I in some kind of danger? Is there someone trying to harm me? I don't understand. That makes me fearful and anxious."

J.C. immediately placed his arm around her and said, "A man's enemies are those of his own house.[70] So, wisdom and understanding of the things that upset **YOU** are the enemies to which you need to be alerted. Things like worry, depression, trauma of any kind, oppression, torment, especially pride and fear—your PERSONAL enemies. These servants are all trained to help you, and they have years of experience."

Suddenly, from behind Serenity came a very young person who skipped right up to J. C., grabbed him around his leg, looked up at him, and giggling, squealed, "Oh, hi J.C. I'm so happy to see you. I meant to be here when you arrived, but got tied up. Sorry. Hi, everybody! Did I miss anything—you know, fun stuff?"—all this in one breath!!

J.C. was not the least thrown off by his antics. He turned to Deborah and, laughing, said, "Deb, this is Joy. He will sometimes sneak up on you like this, sometimes confront you deliberately, and at other times just stay quietly in your house until you notice his presence and laugh with him."

"His job description is to strengthen you, to keep you from grief and depression on a daily basis.[71] His SPECIFIC expertise is in making seemingly awful situations seem less painful as he keeps you buoyed above what is going on around you. He will keep you from growing weary and fainting in your thoughts if you simply let him serve you.[72] Keep in mind that he is of particular discomfort to those who love worry, fear, anxiety, depression, religion, etc. Like everything else, he is a choice. Often, the choice is to follow Joy or become part of another's opinion concerning him. That gets tricky, so look for him when things get upsetting to you or others around you."

By now, Deborah's head was awhirl with all of these things. She felt so concerned that she would not be able to remember all she needed to know to use these servants properly.

"Honey, you have seemed to be afraid of making a mistake and embarrassing yourself, so there is one other servant I want you to know well. Her name is Hope and you met her at the Faith store. She will teach you how to let love encourage you until you know that there is no need ever to be ashamed.[73] Hope will also teach you to completely trust in Father to keep your mind, will, and emotions upbeat and confident.[74] You will soon learn to listen very carefully to what she says and consult her on each process—she will teach you a higher, better way."[75]

Almost in tears, Deborah looked at J.C. and said, "Maybe I don't really need this fine house and all these servants. I could be happy in a cottage—really, I could."

"Only because you have yet to see yourself as I see you."

Deborah opened her mouth to protest more, but instantly Serenity stepped up and took her hand. Turning her head, she said to Grace, "Come on we need to show Deborah her new house."

As they watched them go down the long hallway, Wisdom and Understanding gave each other a high-five at the thought of being privileged to have yet another to join ALL the ones who make up his beautiful Bride.

J.C smiled as he watched the three of them going off to explore Deb's house, an adventure he knew would take a lifetime— a lifetime of experiencing the expertise of these warrior/servants. He paid for her to have these servants to help guide her as each room was cleared of the building debris that had been left there, and then furnished and accessorized appropriately. From behind her, Deb heard a familiar chuckle and her heart danced once more.

A FAMILY REUNION

$\mathcal{S}$oon after moving into the house, J.C. told Deborah he wanted her to meet his family. "It will be a big gathering, so be prepared for a lot of commotion as we're a noisy bunch when we get together," he told her.

"How many people will be there?" she asked.

"So many there will be no way you will meet all of them," he replied.

"How dressy will the reunion be?" she asked. "Shall I wear my new clothes?"

"Honey, you will look wonderful in whatever you wear. My family members will be dressed in many different ways."

"I don't want to embarrass you," Deborah said.

"Why don't you wear the little dress we bought for you at the humility store? You could wear your mercy cape in case you need a wrap," he said.

"I'll find something," she said, "and it won't be that one either."

"Just saying……," J.C. said.

Already getting nervous at the thought of meeting his family; she asked, "When will the family reunion take place?"

"Next Wednesday. They are all excited about our being there with them."

It was Saturday and in spite of his assurance concerning the dress code, Deborah became more and more anxious about what she should wear, her hair, shoes, make up—all the things that interested J.C. the least.[76] He just let her fret, refusing to participate, which only added to her constant anxiety that grew hourly as she listened to the voice of her own insecurity instead of trusting her husband's words to her.

He had said to her, "You are glorious beyond your comprehension. Learn to see yourself through new eyes—MY EYES."

Deborah decided to wear a pair of linen slacks and a tailored blouse. J. C. had said it would be held outside, so she felt this was appropriate. After one more nervous look into the mirror, and again adjusting her hair and clothes; they started for the door.

Deborah stopped, and for the sixth time asked, "Do I look alright?"

"Deb," he said patiently, "You look as beautiful as you did the last time you asked. Now let's go."

Deborah was still uncertain as they approached a large green pasture. There were people EVERYWHERE. It only took a second for Deb to understand why J.C. had said it did not matter what she wore. There were all manner of people in his family!!! People from every kindred, tribe, and tongue were gathered there and everyone was having such fun together.[77]

"These are your **family**?" she asked incredulously! "How did you come to have such a diverse family?"

"Oh, I chose them," he responded, "like I chose you."

There were people in jeans with long hair and beards, people with turbans and long garments, ladies in beautiful saris. There were some with ponchos and boots and she was particularly amazed at those who had on what she considered an inappropriate amount of clothing. "Those shorts are small enough to be a bathing suit," she thought as they walked past a group of young girls. She turned to make a comment about it to J.C., but saw that he seemed quite oblivious to their clothing. "He really does not judge by outward appearances," she thought, and made a mental note to remember that herself.

As they moved through the crowd, there was such a deep appreciation for her husband. She was so proud to be his bride. Looking around at all the mass of people, she thought proudly, "But, **I'm the bride.**"

J.C. was busily greeting and chatting with all the guests and after a while, Deborah began to feel ignored. In order to try and establish her identity for everyone, she began looking for someone who knew her with whom **SHE** could chat. Suddenly, she saw Hope and ran over to her. In her intense desire to be recognized, she forgot that Hope was one of the servants for her house, and asked if Hope remembered meeting her on the visit to the store with J.C. The response almost made Deborah faint from shock and disbelief. "Precious One, He brings so many to me for clothing that I have trouble remembering all of you. Are you enjoying wearing the clothes he helped you choose?"

Hope saw the stunned expression on Deborah's face and knew she needed help with the idea of a many-membered bride. So, putting her arm gently around Deb's shoulders, she began to lead her through the crowd and explain how the needs to supply the work of J.C.'s family were so great that it required brides from every nation, kindred tribe and tongue. At that moment, Righteousness appeared, and the two of them continued to explain to Deborah how J.C. loved every member of his bride with an everlasting love and the Church they made up was one that, as they walked in unity and in the spirit that he exemplified, nothing could prevail against.[78]

Still in a daze, Deborah only nodded in response to the interaction of the two of them. She was unable to speak above the cacophony of questions the angry voices in her brain were screaming! **"Hadn't he chosen *her*? *Why* wouldn't *she* be enough to fulfill his every desire? *SHE* could represent him very adequately on each and every occasion."** With that last thought, her mind traveled to all the places she knew he was represented—large gatherings where she had assumed she would be the center of attention as his bride—now this.

At that moment she realized that Righteousness was saying something to her. "Uh, I beg your pardon," she stammered. He smiled and said, "Deborah, Look at yourself." Surprised, she found they were standing in front of a large mirror. "Oh my," was her response to what she saw. "I thought I looked so beautiful this morning and now…not so much."

Righteousness was now joined by Wisdom who was passing by and heard her pronouncement. Wisdom said, "You are everything you thought yourself to be this morning, Deborah. At least, you were until you started comparing yourself to others and measuring your place in J.C.'s thoughts based on those comparisons. Any time you start to compare who YOU are with who you THINK others are—you become the loser. J.C. would tell you, 'Those who compare themselves among themselves are not wise.'"[79] Righteousness nodded in agreement.

As Wisdom strolled off into the crowd, Righteousness continued, "Deborah as you look at yourself, you see an entire body. It is composed of many members—hands, which need every finger to operate smoothly; legs which need feet, which need toes; eyes to give sight for the hands and feet to move safely; a nose to smell and a mouth to speak, on and on. That is the same design as his bride. There are no more and no less significant ones. In J.C.'s eyes, it is simply his bride, and he is passionately in love with each and every one of you. Just focus on HIM and listen to HIS VOICE as he speaks to you of his love for you. As you hear and abide in this Secret Place with him, you will become so secure in his love that instead of feeling jealousy and rejection toward the other members, you will learn the beauty of unity. No big *I*'s, no little *you's*, simply his Bride, adding to itself one person at a time."

"Well, you may be sure THAT'S going to take me a WHILE," she said.

'What's going to take all that time?" J.C. was suddenly beside her, smiling knowingly.

"It's our little secret, J.C.," Righteousness said over his shoulder as he sauntered off into the crowd.

J.C. tilted her head so that he was looking into her face. His eyes were so full of Love that she suddenly was aware that he knew what she was feeling. She knew her feelings were wrong and knew HE knew they were wrong. However, as she continued to look at the love in his eyes and the smile on his face, those feelings began to fade. NOT GONE, but the smallest glance let her know that continuing to look into him and his love would teach her how to be the bride of his heart and purpose.

"Let's dance," he said.

For the first time, Deborah was aware of the beautiful, beautiful music that was playing. She started looking for the orchestra, and as they danced, she continued looking into the crowd to find the source of the music. Finally, she gave up and decided to just enjoy being close and dancing with J.C. After a moment or two, however, her curiosity overcame her pleasure and she asked, "Where is the orchestra? It must be HUGE."

"Oh it is. You see, Deborah, each person in my bride has his or her own note resonating from within themselves—-instruments for my delight and pleasure. My bride is the orchestra that makes this music in my heart at all times. As each one learns to stay on key and in sync with the others, the music becomes more and more beautiful. Then, once they are well trained, each will be able to hear when his or her note is off key and quickly get back into the flow."

"Can you hear all the sour notes?" Deborah asked.

Laughing, J.C. said, "Sure."

"Does it make you angry?" she asked. J. C. laughed harder.

"Goodness no, the ones with the sour notes are just my child brides, but still golden ones to me." He said.

Now, totally confused and still a bit testy about the 'other brides' thing, "GOLDEN, GOLDEN," she practically screamed. "Why would they be GOLDEN if they can't stay on key? I don't get it."

J.C. smiled, thinking how off key Deborah had been all day, but said, "All my brides are golden to me. They are just at different stages of the process necessary to keep them in perfect tune. All of them are loved equally. However, keeping some of them on key does require a bit more nurturing at times."

"It sounds very unfair to the on-key brides to me," Deborah snapped.

"I see it as an opportunity for them." J.C. said quietly.

"What?" Deborah asked incredulously!

"You see, Deb, love has a light about it and every opportunity to show love to someone in a bad place causes love's light to shine into their darkness; thus blessing them **and** the one showing them love."

"That all SOUNDS great, but not like somewhere I would rush to be," she said.

J.C. was quiet. Finally, realizing he was not going to respond to that, she said, "Sorry if that makes you unhappy. It's just that I can't see myself ever being able to take on that role..... Hmmm, guess that makes me one of your golden child-brides, eh?"

J.C.'s response to this was very tender. "Precious One, that realization shows a rather large degree of maturity. I am excited about your insight." His tenderness melted enough of Deborah's resistance to all of this for her to ask,

"How do you ever change us from being fool-ishly 'golden' into a well-tuned instrument?"

"It's not hard," he said. "I just play the right notes in your ears until your heart can hear and play it back correctly."[80]

Suddenly, Deborah felt very tired—-lots to think about and try to digest. Always aware of her needs, J.C. suggested they should go home and let her get some rest. They turned and waved goodbye to everyone and Deborah had the strangest awareness. **EVERYONE** thought they were dancing with J.C. and **EVERYONE** thought they were leaving with him.

Later, as she drifted off to sleep, she thought, "I wonder if ALL of them now think they are in the arms of their beloved......?"

I DO VS. I WILL

"Yes, Yes, J.C. I do trust that you are right and know what is best for me, but you just don't understand how this works." J.C. always listened quietly as Deborah talked on and on about how wonderful he was and how much she respected and trusted his opinions, and then went on her headstrong way.[81] He smiled and waited patiently for her to realize that this latest venture was not at all what she thought it to be.

He thought of other times that she had walked out of the center of his plans for them only to find herself in over her head, wondering how it all happened the way it did.[82] Smiling, he suddenly remembered the time the neighbors began building the fence over onto their property.

Deborah came to him with the complaint that it was infringing on their rights, and would ruin the beautiful flower bed she had planned for that spot. J.C. had explained to her that the foot of property being taken from them should just be given away kindly and gladly. He seemed to even be GLAD to give it to them![83]

Deborah, on the other hand was furious, first with the neighbor and then with him because he would not do anything about it. "How can you just let this happen to us?" she asked. "It makes me furious that they would presume to just TAKE our property, and you seem to be so delighted with it and a bit intolerant of my wanting to do something about it. After all there are laws and covenants that have to be agreed to and obeyed, you know."

J.C. smiled and said, "Deb, do you really want to talk about LAWS and COVENANTS with me?"

"I don't understand that tone, J.C. It is almost as if you have a different idea than I have of the laws and covenants of our property and you want me to change my mind. I know you are smarter than I am, but I am going to call them and let them know that what they are doing is wrong, and we will have to take legal action if they continue with that fence."

"Two questions Honey: One, what attitude are you going to use to approach them, and two what are you going to do if they refuse to stop?"

"Well, I....I'll just tell them we will have our lawyer contact them. We do have a lawyer, don't we?" Then, suddenly realizing she was going to be in over her head, she turned to J.C. and said, "Besides, why should I have to be the one to handle this? You are the head of this house. You should be the one who attends to this."

"You REALLY want me to be the one who makes this right?"

"Of course you should......," Deborah's voice trailed off as she thought about how J.C. would go about it. "Unless you intend to go over and be nice, and neighborly, and all that P.R. stuff."

"Deborah," J.C. said in a firm, but gentle tone, "you can't have it both ways. Either you do it your way, or I'll do it mine; which, in this case, is a different way from yours."[84]

"J.C., surely your Father's business has a law firm they use. It would be a simple process to just contact them, have them write a letter for us, and not even have to go over there and say anything."

At this, J. C. could no longer keep from laughing. This made Deborah even madder— at him, instead of the neighbors.

"This is not funny, J.C. You are my husband and you are supposed to look after ME and MY interests in everything; be on my side. Instead, you are laughing at me and siding with the ones who are taking FROM me!"

"If you will just sit down, Deborah, I will tell you about our law firm and the letter they would write. Then I will tell you about the Covenants of our company and how they work. When I finish, you will understand that I am not laughing at you, but at the thought of the letter they would receive from our lawyer. It reads very differently from the one you would be expecting them to send."

"In what way?" she asked. "They do know the law about these things, don't they?"

"Yes, they do. However, the law of the Spirit of my Father is very different from the law of the spirit in the world at large.[85] The first law in this instance would be to love one's neighbor as oneself. In which case, their feelings will be as important as yours."[86]

"I just hate this," Deborah said. "It is not fair for them to do this and have you just say we should not make any waves and let them run over us and our property like this."

"We have other choices. We can make war or we can make peace," he said quietly.

"You mean give it to them, don't you?"

"Deborah, one of the laws in my kingdom says, 'What does it profit a man if he gains the whole world and loses his own soul?'[87] Your soul is your mind, your will and your emotions. If you fight this, either way it ends, you lose."

"No, No. If they move it, I can have my flower bed, and they can have their fence- just on their side, not ours," she said.

"Yes, and you will forever have enemies next door. The strife will continually come across that fence to bring its evil works.[88] It will rob your soul to make war over a fence. The things our law firm wars against are not property lines and such.[89] Our war is with things that will kill the soul; things like bad attitudes, emotions, and willfulness, and selfishness. Little things like fences on property lines become insignificant, when we win those wars."

"So what are you going to do?" she asked.

"I am going to contact my Father about the situation, and trust that He will show us how to handle it according to the Law of His Kingdom and it will be done peaceably."[90]

J.C. laughed as he remembered how, a short time later, the phone rang and it was the neighbor. He was saying that he had realized that he was building that fence over too far onto their property, and he wondered if he could just buy that from them rather than tear down the fence that was already finished.[91]

To this, Deborah's immediate response (as he knew it would be) was, "What about my flower bed?"

However, knowing his Father never worked a solution from just one side, J.C. gave Deborah enough time to reflect on what all had been said about the law of Life vs. the law of strife, and in a short time she relented. Many other battles of her mind, will, and emotions came and went to test the marriage Deborah had entered with such joy and confidence that all her troubles were ended. Yet with each battle, she became more of the warrior-bride and less of a child-bride.

There were times when the answer did not come nearly as quickly as the phone call about the fence. Sometimes there were weeks or even years of overcoming to reach the path of a conquered soul, one in which her battles were won by the Life Message laid out by J.C. Deborah, though often weary, was not a quitter. She kept her mind strong by constantly consulting with J. C. Often, unable to reach the high mark he always set for her,[92] she learned obedience through all that she suffered to bring her soul into line with its lover, J.C. With each victory, she would hear that long sought and patiently awaited chuckle.

H.S. IS TO LIVE WHERE??!!

One morning, sometime later; Deb and J.C. were sitting and chatting when J.C. suddenly leaned toward her and said, "Honey, do you remember when we first married, and I was telling you about the gifts I had for you?"

"Yes, do YOU remember my telling you about the one I had hoped it was— round, big, and sparkly?" Deb replied.

J.C. laughed and said, "I remember that vividly. However, that is not the one to which I am referring right now. I am telling you it is time for us to make Holy Spirit feel welcome to live in our house."

"Here, in this house?" Deborah asked in a somewhat astonished tone.

"Yes, here in this house." J.C. replied.

"I don't understand, J.C. We are quite happy here, and things are working with the servants, and—-why would we want to do that? More than that, why would he want to come?"

"Deb, I am more than happy to be here in this house of ours with you. Please don't think otherwise. When H.S. comes, you will never be alone. There will always be someone here to comfort, counsel, help, strengthen, and stand by you no matter where I am."[93]

"What are you saying to me, J.C.? Are you leaving me? If so, nothing you could do or say will ever comfort or strengthen me." Deborah's voice was tinged with terror and her eyes showed how the thought of this frightened her.

"Did I say to you that I would never leave you or forsake you, Deborah?" J.C. asked quietly. Since he had never done this before, Deborah quieted her racing heart and searched his face to try and see what he was thinking. Seeing nothing in his eyes but love and respect, she listened quietly.

J. C. said, "Deborah, you are my Bride. As that, you have come to know and trust me to love, and encourage, and bless you. Your mind, will, and emotions have been loved into a place where they can now be taught how to trust an even deeper love. H.S. will be your teacher."

"I don't understand. Why can't **you** teach me?"

"I HAVE taught you how to **BE** loved and how to overlook, and forgive, and minister to hurts, and play, and have fun. Now it is time for H.S. to do his job which is to guide you into all truth."

"The truth about what— Is there something you haven't told me?"

J.C. laughed and then looked at her with the look that always melted her fears and said, "Deb, Honey, H.S. is my Dad's man who is in charge of Interior Design and Housekeeping. He will do for and with you what you cannot ever do here without him."

"I didn't realize you were so unhappy with my housekeeping and design plans." Deb said in a very defensive tone.

"I am not. I just know that YOU are not happy with some of those rooms that you cannot seem to get designed to please you no matter how hard you have tried and worked to do so."

"I'm working on that, J.C. To exactly what rooms are you referring?"

"The ones to which you have the doors locked so no one can go in and see them. Deb, look at me; Honey, you know what I am saying to you. You need a helper—someone who can see these things more objectively than you can."

"Well, why can't YOU help with it? You married me, and you knew in your heart there would be those rooms. So, it seems to me we don't need to call in somebody else in the family to spread the word around that Deb doesn't know what she is doing."

J. C was quiet for a moment or two and then gently said, "Why don't we leave this for another time and place, a time when you are more open to our talking about it. H.S. would not want to cause strife about his coming here to do these things with you." Deborah, who had turned her back to J.C. so he could not see her tears, turned to respond to that and realized he had quietly left the room.

She sat down and started to weep as she thought about the rooms that were still in disarray and shut up to keep others from seeing her uncertainty and turmoil. After a while, she felt a hand on her shoulder, and thinking it was J.C.; she looked up, ready to apologize and embrace him and willingly agree to his proposal. Instead, Grace was standing there smiling at her and extending her hand to lift her into a standing position.

"Someone wants to see you in the breakfast room, Deborah. I've made some tea for the two of you. Here is a tissue for your tears and nose. Come on in when you are ready."

"Oh, Grace, is it J.C.?"

"No, dearest, it isn't," was all Grace said as she went out the door.

"Who in the world could that be at a time like this? I hope it's not that nosey neighbor. What in the world will she think when H.S. arrives?

Probably spread rumors about us all over the neighborhood. Hope she can't see that I have been crying. Breathe; Breathe......"

Deb busily straightened her blouse and jeans and thought, "J.C. where are you? I don't want to be alone to deal with whomever this is."

When Deborah entered the breakfast room, she was surprised to see Righteousness seated at the table calmly sipping a cup of tea. She was a bit alarmed as she did not quite know how to understand him. She had never figured out his role in her home.

"Good morning!" was his cheerful greeting.

"Good morning, Righteousness," she responded. Then in what she hoped was a tone that denoted her position as owner of the home, she asked, "Did you wish to see me?"

Grace, who was just entering the room with Deborah's tea, almost laughed aloud at the ludicrousness of the scenario she was witnessing. There stood Deborah trying to be more right than Righteousness! Grace dared not look at him lest they both burst into laughter at how ridiculous it all was.

Knowing that laughter was not what Deb needed at that moment; Grace quickly left the room and covered that meeting with belief for Deborah's correction and healing. She had all confidence that as soon as Deborah under- stood Righteousness as a **gift** as opposed to a **judge**; all would be well.

"Actually, I thought **you** needed to see **me**," was his reply.

"There must be some mistake. I didn't ask to see you. I'll call Grace to see what this is about," Deborah responded nervously.

"Deborah, your HEART called out to me for this time with you to assure you of your right- standing in every way with all of the servants and with J.C. You have made a glorious home for J.C. and for all of us."

"Perhaps the one you need to assure of all that is J.C., and I don't know his whereabouts at the moment," she replied.

"Oh, J.C. is very aware of your success as well as how much you are capable of in all areas. YOU are the one who needs to be constantly assured and complimented in order to feel accomplished. What J.C. wants is for you to meet the **real** Deborah—the one <u>we</u> all know and love."

"What do you mean MEET the real Deborah?"

"There is a Person in you who is an exact reflection of the person you have learned to know as J.C. That person needs to be uncovered by H.S. and **seen** by you and others. Deborah, there is a world out there which has no idea of the possibilities available to them. They are in darkness and need to see the light you have seen in J.C."[94]

"How can H.S. do all of this better than J.C.?"

"He will renew your mind so you can see yourself differently. He will show you your unique gifts that are presently hidden behind closed doors."[95]

"There you go bringing those 'closed doors' up to me. J.C. has already pointed those up to me this morning, thank you very much," Deborah quipped sarcastically.

"Deborah, I am one of the gifts H.S. wants to help you understand. You have been given the Gift of Righteousness, but you still insist on keeping those locked rooms that torment you. I am your servant and friend, but you don't understand me as that. You see me as a **JOB** you are constantly trying to 'get right'. When you can begin to see me as who you **ARE**, you can go into those rooms joyfully looking with new eyes at the beautiful change which simply understanding **me** will bring to you. Let H.S., who is noted far and wide for his Interior Design experience, come and complete the work J.C and you have begun so beautifully."

"What about my fear of his Presence here?" Deborah stammered through her tears that were welling up.

About that time, Deborah heard a familiar chuckle. She turned and seeing J.C., ran into his arms. After a while just quietly nestled there, she decided to just abandon herself to a house filled with the Presence of H.S. and allow him to do whatever it was that everyone kept talking about. At this, she heard the familiar chuckle, only to realize it was now her own.

FOR ALL MEN

One morning, the three of them were at breakfast, and as they ate; Deborah suddenly became aware of the beautiful sur-roundings,-the terrace, the grounds, even the fence that the neighbor had built; all stunningly gorgeous.

As this image of her exceptionally good for-tune grew, she suddenly blurted out, "Am I not the most blessed bride anywhere? Look at all of this beauty! My house, my yard, even this food we are enjoying together is so very spe-cial. Thank you J.C., for your provision for me. I just love it!"

J.C. smiled at her and she felt so at peace... until she noticed the glance that he and H.S. exchanged. She had seen that expression before and it always altered things for her. It never occurred to her that these alterations, when understood and walked out, were always helpful. She just immediately became fearful that something in her beautiful world was about to be disturbed by change. At that point, all those fearful thoughts came rushing in to spoil the beauty of her morning. Always perceptive of what was going on inside Deborah's head, J.C. asked, "Is that fear I see on the face that a moment ago was so radiant with joy?"

"I saw that glance that passed between the two of you and wondered if I said or did some-thing wrong," she said.

"Deborah, I love the praises you give me for all the work we have done and are continuing to do here at our home. It blesses me and looks very good on you," J.C. said.[96] "Your expression of joy in all your blessings is particularly special this morning considering the trip H.S. and I have planned for us today."

Deborah once again became excited. The trips that the three of them took were usually such fun and always tended to develop her skills in how to reign as his bride–a position she was learning to enjoy immensely. Trying to get some clue as to what was planned she asked, "Should I have the servants prepare some food for…maybe a picnic?"

"The servants and the food will already be there when we arrive." J.C. said. There was a twinkle in his eye that should have further alerted Deborah, but her excitement caused her to be less observant of J.C. than she should have been.

It all sounded a bit odd to her as she thought she had learned how to order the foods that pleased him, but she just nodded and eagerly asked, "When are we leaving?"

"After breakfast will be fine with me if that is good for you." he said with a smile.

As she said, "OK, that's fine," Deborah just had a strong feeling within her that in reality, it **wasn't** going to be fine. "What is the dress code for this occasion?" Deborah asked, hoping for some clue as to what she should expect the day's excursion to be.

"Whatever you choose, and oh yes, just make sure you include that little shawl we bought at the mercy store," he said. At this, H.S. was so obviously trying not to smile that Deborah became even more apprehensive.

Later, as she dressed, she decided on a lovely suit and some beautiful antique jewelry she had bought one day while shopping. She remembered thinking, "Now this looks like an outfit for the bride of a reigning monarch." As a last minute effort to please J.C., she remembered the "mercy wrap" and casually threw it over her arm.

Downstairs, J.C. and H.S didn't seem to notice all her careful attention to appear regal. A bit disappointed, maybe even testy, she got into the car for their trip. They drove through areas that were totally unfamiliar to Deborah. Finally they entered an area where the houses were so unkempt, the streets were littered with trash, and the people appeared as unkempt as

the houses and the streets. The waste recepta-
cles were overflowing onto the already littered
sidewalks.

Deborah blurted out, "I will be glad when we
get out of here. Obviously, even the people who
pick up the garbage don't want to come here!"

After a few moments of silence in the car J.C.
said, "Deborah, this **is** our destination."

Deborah looked at him in disbelief, waiting
and hoping for the beloved chuckle. When that
did not happen, she turned to H.S. in search
of a denial of any form. What she saw, to her
dismay, was a simple nod of his head. She
looked again at their surroundings. Not only
were the streets littered with trash, there were
people lying around on dirty blankets with little
piles of stuff beside them.

"What in the world would we come here for?
I can't stand this. Why, J.C., if you opened the
door, I am sure there would be a bad odor."

H.S. nor J.C. said anything in response
to this.

"Why is this silence making me so nervous?" Deborah thought.

A bit further into the district, J.C. pulled the car over to the curb and stopped near some particularly disheveled-looking people. Frightened beyond words, Deborah would not look at the people. She just stared straight ahead. What happened next was beyond even her greatest fear—J.C. opened the car door! It was only then that he looked over at her and, without a word; he reached over and took her hand. "This is our adventure, come on Deb."

Deb withdrew her hand and said, "J.C. I always come around to your way and purpose... but **these people**; surely you are teasing. I have on my best suit. One touch from one of them would ruin it. I thought we were coming to some royal event."

"Oh, Deb, **this is** a royal event. To reign in my kingdom, you must learn to be regal in any circumstance and reign from a position of peace and authority over what you see with your eyes and hear with your ears that might not be what

it seems.[97] Deborah, these are my father's subjects too."

"What do you mean 'subjects'?" she asked.

"Well, they are subject to his mercy, his grace,
his loving kindness—all of who he is, just like
you and I are."

At that moment, Deborah saw someone
down the street giving away something that
appeared to be food. "J.C., speaking of Grace,
isn't that her handing that person food?"

"I believe it is." With those words, J.C. opened
the car door, jumped out and began waving to
Grace who smiled and returned his wave.

Deborah turned to H.S. who was still in the car
with her. "Surely Grace knows better than this.
The very idea of her being down here around all
of this and then returning to our house after being
exposed to all of **these people."** Deborah said,
once again emphasizing the "these people" part.

H.S. looked at Deborah and gently said,
"Deborah, do you remember what you were like
before Susan introduced you to J.C.? To our
dad, at times, **your** life probably looked a lot like

these people look to you. They may not have been fortunate enough to have a friend like Susan who just kept insisting they meet J.C., or some of them may have met him and been too busy or challenged by things in their lives to form a relationship with him. Deborah, you are very blessed to have been found before perhaps you wound up like one of 'these people' as you call them. You are learning from J.C. to live from a higher kingdom than they yet understand."

"H.S. there are people who don't want better. "They just want some do—gooder like Grace to come down here and give them something free." Deborah's tone of voice became elevated. "I can't be bothered with people who won't work and help themselves. For your information, I always worked."

Ignoring this recent barrage of words, H.S. continued, "Deborah, it is amazing what reaching beyond **SELF** can do for a hurting world. These few are only a tiny example of the pain that is beyond your carefully guarded boundaries."

"Well," Deborah said sarcastically as she pointed up the street to an older, well groomed gentleman who was speaking intently to a young, scantily dressed girl standing on a corner a short distance away. "He seems to have gotten past his boundaries rather well. I wonder if his wife knows he is an *equal opportunities player*!"

Ignoring how ugly her attitude had become H.S. replied, "As a matter of fact, the person speaking with the young lady across the street IS his wife."

Deborah just stared at the attractive lady and said nothing. "What on earth is all of this about?" she thought.

Continuing, H.S. said, "You see Deborah, their daughter got caught up in drugs and ran away from home. She became a prostitute to support her habit and died as a result of a beating by her pimp. They now sponsor girls for entrance into rehab centers. When the girls are finished at rehab, the couple has established a half-way house where they are taken until they can function on their own.

Deborah watched as they moved quickly down the street speaking to the girls and handing them something she could not see. "What are they handing them, money?" She asked.

"Oh no, it's not money. It is a card with information about how to reach help if they choose to do so."

"I wonder how many of them actually take advantage of it and succeed?" Deborah asked.

"Actually, their success rate has been amazing," H.S. answered.

"How do you know so much about them and their work, H.S.?"

With a chuckle that sounded much like J.C.'s, he said, "My boundaries are extremely open, Deborah."

This remark bypassed Deborah who was intently watching J.C. as he lovingly spoke to, shook hands with, and patted on the back the people she held in such disdain. "He is ENJOYING THEM, just like REAL PEOPLE!" She shivered at the thought. In what seemed an eternity to Deborah, J.C. was back in the vehicle.

He looked questioningly at her and asked, "You are still sure that you won't get out, eh?"

"Not a chance," she retorted.

"Deb, let me ask you something," he said. "If that were me out there on that street, destitute and afraid, would you help **ME**?"

"J.C., what do you mean? You know I would do anything to help you. I will always be there for you," Deborah said as if shocked to be asked this.

"Even if I smelled terrible and dirtied your beautiful suit, you would help me?" he asked.

"J.C., I love you. There is nothing that could keep me from helping YOU, no matter what the circumstances."

"Deb, Honey, when you do for others you **ARE** doing it for **ME**," J.C. said quietly.[98]

"He says very peculiar things at times," she thought, "but I love him anyway."

He chuckled and looked at her with an expression that said, "Even though you don't understand me very well, I love you."

The look was so tender that she was ALMOST sorry she didn't get out of the car for a bit just to please him. Another shiver followed the thought.

REAL PEOPLE

On Sunday morning, Deborah was reading the newspaper when J. C. suggested they not go to their usual place of worship. Deborah was shocked by this and asked, "Is anything wrong? I didn't realize you were unhappy there." He always seemed happy, sharing her enthusiasm for the music, the applause and the rejoicing at this particular church.

"Oh no," J.C. responded, "Nothing there is wrong. I just thought we would try some place different—you know, enlarge our borders!"[99]

"Will H.S. go with us, or will he just go to our regular church?" she asked.

"H. S. is a REAL church-goer. He will be right there with us. Why don't you go up and put on that beautiful suit of yours? I think it will be perfect for today." At this last statement, Deborah's antennae went up. She looked questionably at J.C., but he seemed absorbed in whatever he was doing at the moment. So, saying nothing, she went to get dressed. As she removed the suit from the closet, she thought, "He never tells me exactly what to wear. Hmmm....I wonder......"

An hour later, they left for the "mystery destination." At least, it was a mystery to Deborah. J.C., on the other hand seemed to know exactly where he was going, and H.S. did not seem at all concerned. They rode for almost 30 minutes, chatting about various things along the way. Suddenly, J.C. turned into the parking lot of a huge, gorgeous cathedral. It had beautiful stained glass windows, giant, carved entrance doors, a domed ceiling, and inside, the largest pipe organ Deborah had ever seen. She stood perfectly still—in awe of all its structural details.

At the door they were greeted with a warm welcome and told to sit wherever they chose. "Let's sit here." Deborah said. "That probably isn't a good idea as that pew is where a certain family always sits," J.C. told her.

"Sort of like our church," Deborah whispered smiling as she thought of how she always put her Bible into "her chair" before services.

J.C. smiled and said, "Deb, the location may change, but there are characteristics in people that are the same everywhere whether in a church or out in the world."

Deborah looked around at all the people who were dressed so beautifully and she was glad J.C. had told her to wear the suit. With this thought, she reached over and squeezed his hand. J.C. looked at her, smiled, and nodded as if he knew her thoughts.[100] At that moment, the music began. It was a beautiful prelude, and Deborah was enthralled by the rise and fall of the organ's swells. Tears suddenly formed in her eyes, and when she began to sniff a bit, J.C. handed her his handkerchief. She noticed that she was the only one crying and the lady sitting beside her was glancing her way. She looked at J.C. to get his reaction, but he was not looking at her. She quickly dried her eyes, though she had to staunchly hold back her tears during the remainder of the prelude.

There was prayer, scripture, announcements, an offering, and then the song service began. Deborah always loved this part of the service and was an avid participant. At the only church she had ever attended regularly, the words to the songs were on a screen at the front of the church. Here they were in hymnals, so she hastily found the number listed in the bulletin they had given her upon arrival. She followed along as best she could for a couple of stanzas until she caught onto the different style of music. At that point, she burst forth into enthusiastic and rather loud song. She noticed people smiling, and thought they approved, so she began to sway a bit as she enjoyed singing the beautiful hymns.

After a bit, she realized that people around her were turning and looking at her. They were no longer smiling. "Am I offending these people by my singing?" she wondered. With that thought, she stopped singing and looked around. Everyone was looking at their hymnal, standing very still, and singing quietly. Once again, she looked at J.C. who was behaving like everyone else. He did not look at her, so she looked at her book and fought back tears. This time however, they were not tears of rapture, but of shame. It was so obvious that her accustomed way of worshiping did not fit in here.

When the song service ended, the pastor rose and began his sermon. Deborah always liked to encourage her pastor as he spoke by saying Amen or some other words that let him know she was hearing and agreeing with his message. At the church she attended, this was a fairly common practice which was not considered out of order. She listened intently to the words of the minister. It was a very spiritually—motivating message. He made a statement that particularly blessed her, and she blurted out, "AMEN, yes." At this point, people all over the church turned and looked at her as if they could not believe her behavior.

"Oh, Lord, get me out of here." she thought. Once again, she looked at J.C. for some look of approval, a touch of her hand—ANYTHING!! He just continued to look at the pastor, listening to every word.

FINALLY, the service was over and they rose and started to the door. Some of the people nodded in their direction and a few even spoke to them as they left. Deborah felt their disapproval deep in her heart, and she wanted to shout, "Look at me!! Am I to be ridiculed just because I choose to worship differently?? Does that make me less of a person?"

In the car on the return home, the silence was deafening. When finally, Deborah could stand it no longer she said, "Did I embarrass you at that church? I must have because you would not even look at me. It was as if you did not want those people to know you and I were together." By the time she finished saying all of this, she was in tears.

J.C. did not respond to all of her accusations but, from his seat in the back, H.S. leaned over and brushed her shoulder a couple of times. When she turned and looked at him, he quietly said, "You had something on your pretty suit. I knew you wouldn't want that."

Suddenly, for Deborah the picture became clear. At the church, they had reacted to her just like she reacted to the homeless people. Behavior that was absolutely normal for her was treated with disdain by those to whom it seemed strange—even SINFUL. It now made sense— the new church, "wear your suit", ALL of it.

"J.C., I cannot believe you would set me up like that!! You KNEW they would treat me that way, didn't you? Admit it! You deliberately allowed that to happen to me!!" Deborah's tone of voice was rising with each sentence.

"It may seem that way to you. I can see how it could, but let me ask you something. How successful has my reasoning with you worked in instances where you are determined to see things from a perspective that is different from what I know as best and true?" J.C. asked. "For instance, today, the people who, in your mind, were dressed and behaved appropriately are now THOSE PEOPLE just as the homeless were the other day."

Deborah thought for a minute of two. Suddenly, she remembered the burlap dress that was all about forgiveness, the food at the restaurant, the family reunion, the fence, and several more instances when this was exactly the situation.[101] "So, I still don't see how it could make you allow me to be so humiliated."

"You always see things better from an experiential standpoint. Today, you experienced shame, which is always rooted in pride. Had you not needed the approval of those people, you would have continued to worship without any shame or consideration of who was looking. We are created for worship and praise, and you were just being who you are and worshiping as you understand. They, in turn, were being and worshiping as they understand. Both of you failed to receive the blessing of the moment because the **mis**understanding of your personal value allowed the opinions and behavior of others to overwhelm the **under**standing of that value.

"In the same way, many of my people continue to live with less abundance than has been made available to them. It seems they value their own shame or other's opinions above their Creator's ability. They then give up on who they are and live out of their lesser self. Deborah, I don't judge you, the homeless, or THOSE people. I simply set you free to become all you can be and then, I love you wherever you are."

Still being the "old" Deb, she tried accusing him once more. "Well, the least you could have done was LOOK at me, not just leave me hanging out there like someone unknown to you. Why did you do that?"

J.C. suddenly chuckled and said, "Well, Honey, everybody else in the church was looking at you, so I just figured you didn't need another pair of eyes staring at you."

From the back seat, Deb heard a little laugh. At first it made her angry. However, after thinking about how ridiculous she looked and sounded in the midst of that service, she too laughed and jokingly slapped him on his arm. At that they all laughed heartily and enjoyed the drive back home. Later that afternoon, Deb said to them, "I just have one more thing to say about this morning."

With a chuckle, J.C. said, "Honey I don't think either of us ever doubted that."

Dismissing this with a wave of her hand, Deborah said, "I can now see that I certainly was judgmental and haughty when we went to visit the homeless people. I not only misunderstood THEM, I misunderstood how my staying in the car made them feel, and how it made you feel, J.C. I did not support your generous efforts to help less fortunate people, and I would like you to know I am sincerely sorry. Feeling judged in the same way taught me a BIG lesson today that, though painful, I will not soon forget. Your love is changing me, J.C. So, I can see how that kind of love should pour out onto them as well. Will you forgive me for being stubborn and headstrong?" As if joking, he said, "Only if you throw in the pride."

"Yeah, I guess that was really at the root of all of it, wasn't it so, O.K., the pride too."

"You are forgiven. Besides, I think this little adventure might just make that dress fit better." He said, giving her a hug.

From an easy chair in the corner, they heard, "WHEW, I'm glad **that** is all finished. Now could we talk about something more pleasant....like dinner?"

"Not until you forgive me too. Your sitting in the car with me was so comforting, but unfair to you, J.C., and the others," she said.

"Oh, I forgave that in the car. Sooo, if that will work for you, we're good here."

This brought a corporate chuckle as they all walked out to the kitchen to forage for something to eat.

"LIVING" ROOMS

As Deborah worked in her house with H.S., she gained a deep respect for his understanding and his quiet way of guiding her into truth[102] about the rooms they were redecorating—or actually cleaning out would be a better term.

Deborah laughed as this thought triggered how, as J.C. first brought it up, she had been so happy to think about the arrival of H.S. Then, she had reacted so negatively to J.C.'s announcement that she was going to have his help getting all those locked rooms into order. "Strange," she thought, "how of lack of understanding keeps causing me, to fight the very things I need most."[103]

She remembered the fight with Righteousness. She had worked so hard for years to be like him—and failed. All of this to the point of avoiding him completely, at least until H.S. showed her how to **receive him** as.....well, sort of a "housewarming" gift from J.C.[104] It was as if a box containing who she really was had opened. In it were the treasures of a new vision—vistas of possibility![105] Even her intimate moments with J.C. took on a new freedom to express her innermost concepts of love, thankfulness, even doubt!

It was such a relief not always struggling to "**BE**" what she thought of as righteousness, and realize that the person she now saw was a reflection of who she **was BE-coming** as J.C.'s bride!! As H.S. taught her how to rethink this, and live out of a "Righteousness Reflection," she found herself behaving more like what she saw in that reflection, as opposed to always struggling in her own limited efforts! "Oh what a relief it is," Deborah sang as, sitting on the patio, she reflected on how much she and H.S. had accomplished in her house since his arrival—lots of stuff was now gone—shaken up, thrown out, and redeveloped by his expert guidance.[106]

"No wonder he is in charge of the Interior Design Department of our company." Deborah was suddenly aware of the referral to 'our' company. She had never thought of herself as a partner with Father, J.C., and H. S. in their company.

"Oh my, yet another new reflection, I will just have to meditate on that and let H.S. give me more understanding of my place in their company, or kingdom as they call it."

H.S. interrupted her meditations as he appeared on the patio with a big smile on his face. "Good morning, Lady," he greeted her.

"H.S. whenever I see you, you are always smiling. Your happy Presence here blesses me more than I can say."

"Thank you Deborah, I love being welcomed and embraced as your friend, confidant, and designer to comfort and encourage you. I appreciate the courage it takes to welcome into your home someone you have previously not known and understood completely. I admire you for trusting J.C.'s gift to you of my expertise in.....well really, in showing HIM to you more clearly."[107]

She replied, "Well, I thought I knew him well, but I am learning to trust what you say to me. I mean...what's not to love about getting to know J.C. even better? It's a lesson **anyone** would be certain to love."

H.S. laughed at the new Deborah. He had only been working with her on her house for a short time, and she was learning to hear from him and trust him more and more each day.

"Are you ready to tackle that upstairs today?" he asked.

Deborah hesitated, she would soooo rather just sit here in his Presence and listen to him talk in that quite, gentle voice. At the thought of this, Deb seemed to drift into a peaceful assurance that no matter what was in those rooms, H.S. would lead her through them. Grinning, Deborah looked at H.S. and said, "Why am

I grinning like this when we both know that I DREAD this?"

"Gracious, is there a room upstairs where 'Dread' lives?" H.S. asked. "If so, we need to redo that one immediately. 'He' may be one of the main reasons you haven't been able to conquer ANY of those rooms."[108]

At this bit of insight, she remembered how, when starting in a room, she would be filled with dread, then with a feeling of inadequacy. Finally, she would just give up, close the door, and quit.

"You know H.S.; you may have hit on a clue to my CONSTANT feeling of inadequacy. Now, that I think of it, maybe that is why I sometimes react negatively to J.C.'s instruction and teasing."

"Let's go up and visit 'Dread's' room, it sounds as if it is a big mess." H.S. said good—naturedly.

As they went up to the top floor, Deborah began to imagine she heard, "Are you REALLY going to let him see into all the mess you have crammed into these rooms? There are years of junk in there. You know he will tell J.C. Or even worse, what if he tells J.C.'s dad? That will wind up the partnership in the company or kingdom or whatever." At this Deborah's pace slowed.

"Now, you aren't getting tired already, are you? We haven't started yet," H.S. teased.

"No, I just hate for you to see what is inside these rooms," she said.

"Deborah, I did not come here to JUDGE these rooms. I came to FIX them. I promise, you are going to be so happy when we finish that you will feel like a different person. For the first time, you are going to really LIKE your house. It is going to be the house J. C. showed you as you were walking that day long ago. Let's make it a treasure hunt of sorts."

She laughed at the thought of how shocked he was going to be at the "treasures" in those rooms.

"Let's go in here first," H.S. said.

Hesitating, Deborah realized how she dreaded opening that particular door. Then she became aware of "Dread". "So this must be 'his' room!" she thought.

"All I need is permission, Deb. I have the entry key from J.C."

"I'll close my eyes…OK. Open it," she said.

"Oh no," H.S. said gently. "It won't work that way. If you refuse to recognize how 'dread' appears, you cannot see him as he is. If you cannot see **HIM** as he is, you will always believe **YOURSELF** to be as he is. **That,** Dear One, is the lie."

"It is just so HARD to look at this mess and realize it is here in MY HOUSE…..for such a long time too!"

H. S. smiled and said, "Well, then this is MY job and I <u>LOVE</u>, not DREAD it! When you look at this room, you just see piles of stuff. When I look at it, I see piles with names on them."

"REALLY?" Deborah said, staring hard at the stacks and trying to see what he saw.

"You could divide this into 3 large piles that represent the links of a chain that ties you in a place in which you cannot achieve. Not only can you not achieve getting rid of this clutter, but you also are hindered in achieving your life's goals.

"Oh," Deborah said weakly.

"OUCH would be a better description of the pain dread causes. You see the pile over there? It has 'procrastination' written on it. If I weren't here as your teacher/designer, would you tackle this or promise 'Dread' to take care of it very soon?"[109]

"I think you know the answer to that," she said.

"Deborah, I am not condemning you. That isn't how I teach. Instead, I am going to unveil the darkness of dread, and the Light of Understanding will swallow it up."[110]

"Let's start with this pile," H.S. said. "We have named it 'PROCRASTINATION'. It has several dark places. First of all, it is a liar. We have both heard J.C. tell us who is the father of lies.[111] He isn't the same Father as the CEO of our company and lying is his native language. So you are being lied to by a professional who says to you, 'someone else would understand how to do that, but you don't'; or, 'that will never work'; or, 'that is stupid and YOU are stupid'; 'be ashamed'; etc."

"Oh, I've heard ALL of the above." Deb said.

"The second dark place is in the pit where these messages dig a place for you to live. Every time you give in and agree with their darkness, the pit gets deeper. Finally, you are in so deep, and it becomes so dark that you can't see a way out. The pit that dread has dug for you has a name. Its name is PITY. The deeper you sink into its mire of pitying yourself, the less power you have to climb out of the pit it has dug. Pity is all about not knowing the POWER SOURCE whose entire life's ambition is to give **you** Power to overcome your dread and live above it.[112] So, the choice is: Am I going to be Pitiful or Powerful?"[113]

As H.S. was speaking to her, each pile seemed to grow less daunting. They would shrink at the sound of his voice and decrease in his Presence. Deborah was awestruck at how well he knew her and how to diminish her problem of hoarding destructive forces![114]

"This pile represents one of the most dangerous stages of dread. Its name is 'Guilt'.

Another name for it is UNFORGIVENESS. Guilt is the worst kind of unforgiveness. Its aim is always destruction. The MO it uses is constantly demanding performance from you and others in order to pay the price necessary to assuage and pacify its cravings. Guilt always demands payment from something or somebody to assuage its appetites. When the performances are not staged, the unforgiveness you are already feeling is reinforced, thus digging the pit even deeper.

Deb, understand that, first you must forgive yourself and then you can forgive others. The guilt assigned to yourself robs you of relationships, and unforgiven people can hurt you when they are not even <u>thinking</u> about you. The same is true of the guilt attached to unforgiven circumstances; it will continue to erode the pit long after the events are in the past."

Suddenly, as H.S. was speaking, there atop the large guilt/unforgiveness pile with all of its resentment, bitterness, anger, and turmoil sat Grace and Righteousness. They were just sitting there in the middle of all of its YUK as if awaiting an invitation to dive in!!

"We thought you might need some help," Grace said.

H.S. laughed. "I was wondering when my reinforcements were going to show up."

Deborah was stunned. "How did they get in here? Why haven't they already cleaned it up?" she wondered. Then, "No guilt transferred to them—this is MY problem, and I have not sought their services in handling it!" With that thought, she suddenly saw that pile shrink even more.

"Deborah," Righteousness said, "J.C. paid a huge price for us to serve you by helping to clean up this and all of your other rooms. However, in spite of the fact that J.C. has given the keys to your rooms to H.S.; the final say for unlocking the doors is yours. As long as they are locked, we have no authority to show YOU how to let US be the 'Clean-Up-the- Darkness-Crew.'" As they were laughing at this analogy, Grace threw open the heavy draperies, and brilliant light flooded the room. Deborah gasped at

the difference the light made on everything—
even the piles of stuff looked less daunting than
before. "Honey, learn all you can about us and
how to use us to empower YOU in the way J.C.
has paid for and provided."

Deb realized she could now walk in this
room unhindered by the fear of Dread's clutter.
When Grace threw open those heavy draperies
and allowed light to flood every area, she felt a
freedom akin to the one she had felt on that first
day as she and J.C. looked at their new home.
Her new awareness of all the help available to
her, and all the light on everything caused H.S.
to be able to make quick work of putting the fin-
ishing touches on this room and bringing it to
perfection.

Day after day, month after month, room after
room; H.S. and Deborah cleaned, repaired
damage, and brought perfect restoration to
each area. Always, in each room's clearing,
Grace, Righteousness, Hope, and Joy would
come in to make the process move with pre-
cision and bring it to perfection. Their Love

overwhelmed each project and made Deborah increasingly courageous about getting finished with her house.[115]

The hallway that connected ALL of the rooms was quite long. On one occasion, as they were going from one room to another Deborah looked up at H.S. and said, "This hallway is so long and dark. It goes all the way back to the beginning of this house and it gives me the creeps too. I wonder why?"

"By 'creeps', I assume you mean that it makes you fearful, right?"

"I never thought of it that way, but yes—fearful, that's it."

"Fear is at the bottom of **all** clutter, Deb. It hides in the darkness so that it is not seen or suspected as the root problem. It parades itself as truth and makes error look like the solution. It makes things look "good", but good is not your goal. LIFE is—a life that that knows Truth and Freedom; a new freedom that will eliminate fear, dread, procrastination and guilt with all of their combined tentacles."

Deborah thought of J.C.; how he was always right, always faithful, always patient, always the same.[116] "He is truly exceptional in every way," she thought. Her thoughts of their love became so intense that she said aloud, "J.C. **IS** that Life to me."

Joy began to dance and clap at this announcement and H. S. said, "You are designed to be just like J.C., perfect in all your ways." So, let's get finished with these last rooms." H.S. chuckled as he turned to walk down the hall.

"You sound just like J.C.," Deborah said.

"And YOU are getting the big picture, My Dear."

"What do you mean by that?" she asked.

"I mean that when Love becomes your motivator, all the things you and I have been dealing with, have to leave. Nothing unpleasant can stay in the Presence of Love."

"H.S., that is exactly the way I feel whenever I am with J.C. It is as if nothing can harm me and nothing is wrong in my world. I am just **LOVED**, in spite of my mess. His Love is so constant and strong that it just overpowers who I am and whatever I am doing at the moment and takes me over."

Stopping in mid-sentence and wheeling to face H.S.; she said, "Do you know what I mean?"

H.S. looked at her with loving amusement and said, "I think I just might get it."

At that very moment, J.C. appeared at the end of the hallway. With a squeal, Deborah ran into his arms and started talking a mile a minute about all the progress being made. J.C. listened, smiling and encouraging her enthusiasm in the progress report.

Deborah, with a sudden change of expression looked anxiously at H.S. and then, turned to J.C. She said in a somewhat anxious tone, "I didn't even ask how long you are going to be here H.S. You won't leave until our project is finished, will you? I mean, I just love the job you, Grace, Righteousness, and the others have done thus far."

Relief and joy flooded her face when J.C. answered for H.S. and said, "Honey, we are here for you and we have no plans to ever leave you. H.S. has stayed with projects much larger and more tedious than yours, so I feel certain he won't leave you."[117]

"WHEW, that is good news. Come on H.S.; let's show him how beautiful his home is becoming now that you are helping here." Deborah said as she danced down the hall toward her finished goals. Behind her, J.C. and H.S. gave each other a high-five. Already a long way down the hall, Deborah thought with a grin, "Are they both chuckling at me?"

THE MYSTERY REVEALED

*D*eborah and J. C. loved walking and talking together. One afternoon during such a time, J.C. said, "You know, Honey, Dad loves for you to come and visit him, and I am glad you are doing that more often these days."

Deborah did not answer, but thought of all the years she had just not felt comfortable going to see his dad. J.C. gave her time to respond and then continued. "He thinks you have a grasp of the kingdom he has prepared for you and how to operate with excellence in your position there."

Deborah still remained quiet for some time as she thought about what J.C. had just said to her. It seemed she could not feel this to be the truth. However, she HAD LEARNED to believe whatever J.C. said as absolutely factual. This prompted her to say, "J.C., why can't I feel as if he loves and enjoys my company as much as you say he does?"

"Perhaps your interpretation of 'Father' is distorted. When we married, he became **your** father in the same way he has always been mine. All of his goodness, all of his love, all of his blessings, all that he is and has, became yours. That is how he wants you to understand him. Why don't you just ask him to open the eyes of your heart and reveal himself in this way?"[118]

"How long do you think it will take for me to have that heart, J.C.?"

He smiled and said, "As long as it takes you to start believing that you **already** have it."

Deborah was determined to find her "father heart". She began to visit Dad more and more often. At times, she would think she had it down to a science and at others, she would think, "Not so much, today." This went on for some time.

Finally, she said to J.C., "You know, I don't think I have a heart like you told me I should have."

"Did I say SHOULD have, or COULD have?" J.C. asked.

"Well, what's the difference? It seems the same to me." She thought for a while, and suddenly said, "Oh, now I see what you mean. 'SHOULD' have presents an obligation. 'COULD' have presents an opportunity!!" She exclaimed. This brought the chuckle she had come to under-stand as a loving indicator of approval.

He said lovingly, "Honey the next time you go to visit Dad, go joyfully. Go, being thankful that he is so accepting of you just as you are. See him as one presenting you with opportu-nities to be even more than you can now see. The way you go in to visit him is how you will leave feeling about your visit. If you enter his gates thankfully, you will give him praise and worship him with thanksgiving.[119] In return, you will receive praise from him to have and give to others."

Deborah did not respond immediately, so J.C. continued. "Think about it, Deb, when you go to visit Dad remember, he only sees <u>you</u> as a part of <u>me</u>, and that brings him great joy. The next time you go, try to see how much joy **your visit** brings to **his heart**. That will make your visit joyful and glorious."[120]

Deborah began to ask H.S. to visit Dad with her, and in time, she and H.S. would go in together laughing and praising Dad for all the many things that were happening in her part of his kingdom—things too great for her imagination to comprehend.

On the way to visit one day, she said to H.S., "You know I am just overwhelmed by the things Dad is showing me about his kingdom. It is just more than I can wrap my mind around. I truly feel like I should have some part in the workings of it, but it is so huge that I just can't ever see myself fitting into it as I would like."

"I have an idea." H.S. said. "Today, why don't you ask him to give you a vision of your place in his plan of action?"[121]

"Give me a what—a vision?" She laughed. "Isn't that something you see that isn't really happening?"

"If Dad gives you a vision, it is already happening in **HIS** realm. You just trust what he is showing you and **HE** will bring it to pass."[122]

"It cannot be that simple, can it?" She asked.

"Simple may not be the best terminology, but you see, Deb; Dad never begins something he cannot and will not bring to completion."[123]

Deborah could hardly wait for her own personal vision of how she fit into this wonderful, but mysterious kingdom. She asked Dad about it and, to her surprise, he was thrilled at the prospect of her becoming an active agent—of—participation in his purposes. He said, "Deb, Honey, you just stay in my presence in your heart and mind. There, you will begin to see and hear directions, and when you hear them, follow them."

Gradually, she was becoming an enthusiastically intense believer in everything Dad said to her. Her visits were entered into with a new joy and with ecstatic praise for the privilege of being part of such royalty.[124] Deborah began to listen intently for the "voice behind her."[125]

She learned the value of just sitting quietly in his Presence. This became one of her favorite times with Dad. It was a time of just experiencing the love that emanated from his being and letting the intensity of it radiate through her being. She learned to receive from him at a cellular level that elevated her body's and her mind's performances to new levels of excellence. It was so marvelous that she spent more and more time just basking in the love and then leaving for her day's tasks with increased vigor and joy.

One day while shopping, she ran into Susan. They were so glad to see each other and decided to have lunch and catch up on the last few months of each other's lives. During lunch, Susan began to tell Deborah about the Bible study that was meeting at her apartment. When she finished all the wonderful accounts of things the study group were experiencing together, she invited Deborah to come join them. Deborah was on the verge of saying no, when she heard a quiet voice inside saying, "Yes, go, Deborah." She readily accepted and made certain of the date and time. As they parted, Deborah felt that she had received a vision for a part in Dad's plan.

As she began attending, she was able to share with the other girls how she not only studied his word, but how she visited with him and just sat in his Presence to absorb his love and hear his words of instruction on how to love others. At first, they were not too keen on this new approach to the one she knew as Dad. They questioned the fact that she said he would actually TALK to her. However, as time passed and Deborah's love was not offended by their lack of understanding, they began to feel free in her presence and started asking questions. She let the love that had been deposited into her exude onto them and, before long, they became a GROUP of lovers. Neighborhoods were changed as the love they were experiencing flowed into them. A Love that was without faultfinding; a Love that did not judge—it just LOVED.

One of the ladies introduced Deborah to a young pastor and his family. He too, loved others deeply and was so dedicated to the vision for ministry he believed God had called him to accomplish. Oddly enough, it was to the homeless of the community. He and Deborah had long discussions about their journeys on the path of love they now were able to walk more comfortably.

After one such visit with him, as Deborah walked away, she heard, "He needs money. His family does without necessities a lot of times." Deborah, who had one day asked Dad for a giver's heart, asked H.S. how she should go about meeting that need. Thrilled by her request, he worked out a way to get money and other needs to the family without their ever knowing Deborah was involved. She loved it when H.S. began to refer to her as a "Secret Agent" of Dad's love and plan for supply to that young family and others with whom he placed her in contact.

H.S said one day as they were joking about her being the "agent" and his being the "private eye" who found those in need, "Dad was, after all, the originator of abundant giving. He did not hold back all that he had."[126]

After a bit, she said, "Yes, and Precious J.C. took what Dad gave and regifted it to all of us.... SOOO AMAZING."

As days, months, and years passed, Deborah learned how to REST in the Love she was receiving.[127] Her ministry grew and blossomed in areas she would have never suspected she could be used. She prayed, taught people, gave her money to people, listened to the hearts of others, and brought peace to turmoil; on and on. All with the understanding that it was because of J.C. and his family's nurturing her back from a deep pit.

In the meantime, she met with Dad often and had such fun praising him as she told him about all of the connections she was making and the absolute assurance she had in his provision for all the plans of her "agency". They both laughed at this analogy. "Dad," she said one day, "the most fun of all is coming to visit you and sharing everything that is happening and how blessed I am to have finally learned to **just flow in the love** instead of always striving to swim upstream in the river of doubt and suspicion." They laughed together when Dad said, "You think YOU are glad."

In the years to come, the ears of Deborah's heart became more and more in tune with that of Dad until she barely knew the sound of his heart from that of her own. One day as she was just basking in the glory of his Presence, Dad said to her, "Deb, more and more, you are taking on the image of my son, J.C."

She knew it was a compliment, but did not understand it. She decided instead of asking, to just meditate on it and see what she found in her heart. However later, as they were dining together, she decided to relate the conversation to J.C. and ask what he thought it meant. J.C. was silent for a moment while he looked at her with such adoration that her heart almost stopped. Then, he reached and took her hand as he said quietly, "It means, my dearest Bride, that you are uncovering the solution to the mystery of the ages—which is; I in you, you in me, and the two of us in Father. We are finally becoming ONE."[128] With this, he gave her a hug and once again, a loving chuckle.

SCRIPTURE REFERENCES

(Comments in quotes inserted by author)

1. *Matthew 16:13-17: "Now when Jesus went into the region of Caesarea Philippi, He asked his disciples, Who do people say that the Son of Man is? And they answered, Some say John the Baptist, others say Elijah, and others Jeremiah or one of the prophets. He said to them, But who do you (yourselves) say that I am? Simon Peter replied, You are the Christ, the Son of the Living God."*

2. *Psalm 23:2-3: "He makes me to lie down in (fresh, tender) green pastures: He leads me beside the still and restful waters. He*

*refreshes and restores my life (myself):
He leads me in the paths of righteous-
ness (uprightness and right standing with
Him—not for my earning it, but) for His
Name's sake."*

3. *Psalm 118:1: "Oh give thanks to the Lord,
for He is good: for His mercy and lov-
ing-kindness endure forever."*

4. *Malachi 3:6a: "For I am the Lord, I do not
change."*

5. *Philippians 4:19: "And my God will lib-
erally supply (fill to the full) your every
need according to His riches in glory in
Christ Jesus."*

6. *Philippians 3:10: "(For my determined
purpose is) that I may know Him (that I
may progressively become more deeply
and intimately acquainted with Him, perceiving and recognizing and understanding the wonders of His Person more
strongly and more clearly), and that I may
in that same way come to know the power
outflowing from His resurrection (which it*

exerts over believers), and that I may so share His sufferings as to be continually transformed (in spirit into His likeness even) to His death, (in the hope) that if possible, I may attain to the (spiritual and moral) resurrection, (that lifts me) out from among the dead (even while in the body)."

7. Romans 2:4: "Or are you (so blind as to) trifle with and presume upon and despise and underestimate the wealth of His kindness and forbearance and long suffering patience: Are you unmindful or actually ignorant (of the fact) that God's kindness is intended to lead you to repent (to change your mind and inner man to accept God's will?"

8. Song of Solomon 2:10-13: "My beloved speaks and says to me, Rise up, my love, my fair one, and come away. For, behold, the winter is past: the rain is over and gone. The flowers appear on the earth: the time of the singing (of birds) has come, and the voice of the turtledove is heard in

the land. The fig tree puts forth and ripens her green figs and the vines blossom and give forth their fragrance. Arise, my love, my fair one, and come away."

9. Job 36:22: "Behold God exalts and does loftily in His power; who is a ruler or a teacher like Him?"

10. Romans 5:17: "For if because of one man's trespass (lapse, offense) death reigned through that one, much more surely will those who receive (God's) overflowing grace (unmerited favor) and the free gift of righteousness (putting them into right standing with Himself) reign as kings in life through the one Man Jesus Christ (the Messiah, the Anointed One)."

11. Zephaniah 3: 17: "The Lord thy God is in the midst of you, a mighty One, a Savior (Who saves). He will rejoice over you with joy: He will rest (in silent satisfaction) and in His love He will be silent and make no mention (of past sins, or even recall them): He will exult over you with singing."

12. Psalm 23:5: "You prepare a table before me in the presence of my enemies. You anoint my head with oil, my (brimming) cup runs over."

13. Proverbs 3:24: "When you lie down, you shall not be afraid; yes, you shall lie down, and your sleep shall be sweet."

14. Psalm 39:6: "Surely every man walks to and fro—like in a pantomime surely for futility and emptiness he is in turmoil; each one heaps up riches, not knowing who will gather them."

15. Matthew 6:34: "So do not worry or be anxious about tomorrow, for tomorrow will have worries and anxieties of its own. Sufficient for each day is its own trouble."

16. 2 Corinthians 10:12b: "However, when they measure themselves with themselves, and compare themselves among themselves, they are without understanding and behave unwisely."

17.   Psalm 51:7: "Purify me with hyssop and I shall be clean (ceremonially): wash me, and I shall (in reality) be whiter than snow."

18.   Matthew 5:37: "Let your Yes be simply Yes, and your No be simply No; anything more than that comes from the evil one."

19.   1 John 4:18: "There is no fear in love (dread does not exist), but full grown (complete, perfect) love turns fear out of doors and expels every trace of terror! For fear brings with it the thought of punishment, and (so) he who is afraid has not reached the full maturity of love (is not yet grown into love's complete perfection)."

20.   Jeremiah 1:5: "Before I formed you in the womb, I knew and approved of you (as my chosen instrument) and before you were born I separated and set you apart consecrating you; (and) I appointed you as a prophet to the nations."

21.   Colossians 3:3: "For (as far as this world is concerned) you have died and your (new real) life is hidden with Christ in God."

22. Matthew 15:6: "So for the sake of your traditions (the rules handed down by your forefathers), you have set aside the Word of God (depriving it of force and authority and making it of no effect)."

23. 1 Corinthians 13:4-7: "Love endures long and is patient and kind; love never is envious nor boils over with jealousy, is not boastful or vainglorious, does not display itself haughtily. It is not conceited (arrogant and inflated with pride): it is not rude (unmannerly) and does not act unbecomingly. Love (God's love in us) does not insist on its own rights or its own way for it is not self—seeking: it is not touchy or fretful or resentful: it takes no account of the evil done to it (it pays no attention to a suffered wrong)."

24. Ephesians 5:25: "Husbands love your wives, as Christ loved the church and gave Himself up for her."

25. *Psalm 37:4: "Delight yourself also in the Lord, and He will give you the desires and secret petitions of your heart."*

26. *Acts 2:25: "For David says in regard to Him, I saw the Lord constantly before me for He is at my right hand that I may not be shaken or overthrown or cast down (from my secure and happy state)."*

27. *Hebrews 11:1: "Now faith is the assurance (the confirmation, the title deed) of the things (we) hope for, being the proof of things (we) do not see and the conviction of their reality (faith perceiving as real fact what is not revealed to the senses)."*

28. *Galatians 5:6: "For (if we are) in Christ Jesus, neither circumcision nor uncircumcision counts for anything, but only faith activated and energized and expressed and working through love."*

29. *Isaiah 61:3: "To grant (consolation and joy) to those who mourn in Zion—to give them an ornament (a garland or diadem) of beauty instead of ashes, the oil of joy*

instead of mourning, the garment of praise instead of a heavy, burdened, and failing spirit—that they may be called oaks of righteousness (lofty, strong, and magnificent, distinguished for uprightness, justice, and right standing with God), the planting of the Lord, that He may be glorified."

30. *Psalm 33:1: "Rejoice in the Lord, O you (uncompromisingly) righteous (you in right standing with God): for praise is becoming and appropriate for those who are upright (in heart)."*

31. *Psalm 25:6: "Remember, Oh Lord your tender mercy and loving—kindness: for they have been ever from of old."*

32. *Lamentations 3:22-23: "It is because of the Lord's mercy and loving—kindness that we are not consumed, because His (tender) compassions fail not. They are new every morning; and abundant is Your stability and faithfulness."*

33. *Colossians 3:12: "Clothe yourselves therefore, as God's own chosen ones*

(His own picked representatives, (who are) purified and holy and well beloved (by God Himself), by putting on behavior marked by tenderhearted pity and mercy, kind feeling, a lowly opinion of yourselves, and gentle ways, (and) patience (which is tireless and long suffering, and has the power to endure whatever comes, with good temper)."

34. *Matthew 27:18: "For He knew that it was because of envy that they had handed Him over to them."*

35. *Mark 15:29-30: "And those who passed by kept reviling Him and reproaching Him in harsh and insolent language wagging their heads and saying, Aha, you Who would destroy the temple and build it again in three days, Now rescue Yourself (from death), coming down from the cross! So also the chief priests, with the scribes, made sport of Him to one another, saying, He rescued others (from death); Himself He is unable to rescue."*

36. Luke 23:34: "And Jesus prayed, Father, forgive them, for they know not what they do. And they divided His garments and distributed them by casting lots for them."

37. Hebrews 8:11: "And it will nevermore be necessary for each one to teach his neighbor and his fellow citizen or each one his brother, saying, Know (perceive and have knowledge of, and get acquainted by experience with) the Lord for all will know Me, from the least to the greatest."

38. John 3:16: "For God so greatly loved and highly prized the world that He (even) gave up His only begotten (unique) Son, so that whoever believes in (trusts in, clings to, relies on) Him shall not perish, (come to destruction, be lost) but have eternal (everlasting) Life."

39. Psalm 103:2-5: "Bless (AFFECTIONATELY, gratefully praise) the Lord, O my soul; and all that is (deepest) within me, bless His holy name! Bless the Lord (affectionately, and gratefully praise) the Lord, O my soul,

and forget not (one of) all His benefits. Who forgives (every one of) all your iniquities. Who heals (each one of) all your diseases. Who redeems your life from the pit and corruption, Who beautifies, dignifies, and crowns you with loving kindness and tender mercy; Who satisfies your mouth (your necessity and desire at your personal age and situation) with good so that your youth, renewed, is like the eagle's (strong, overcoming, soaring)."

40. *Luke 6:38: "Give and (gifts) will be given to you; good measure, pressed down, shaken together, and running over will they pour into (the pouch formed by) the bosom of (your robe and used as a bag). For with the same measure you deal out (with the measure you use when you confer benefits on others) it will be measured back to you."*

41. *Luke 23:43: "And He answered him, truly I tell you, today you shall be with me in Paradise."*

42. *1 Peter 3:3-4: "Let not yours be (merely) external adorning with (elaborate) inter-weaving and knotting of the hair, the wearing of jewelry, or changes of clothes; But let it be the adorning and beauty of the hidden person of the heart, with the incorruptible and unfading charm of a gentle and peaceful spirit, which (is not anxious or wrought up, but) is very precious in the sight of God."*

43. *Galatians 5:22-23: "But the fruit of the (Holy) Spirit (the work which His presence within accomplishes) is love, joy (gladness) peace, patience (an even temper, forbearance), kindness, goodness (benevolence), faithfulness, gentleness (meekness, humility), self-control (self-restraint, continence). Against such things there is no law (that can bring a charge)."*

44. *Galatians 5:1: "In this freedom, Christ has made us free (completely liberated us); stand fast then, and do not be hampered*

and held ensnared and submit again to a yoke of slavery (which you have once put off)."

45. Romans 8:1-2: (MSG) "With the arrival of Jesus, the Messiah, that fateful dilemma is resolved. Those who enter into Christ's being here for us no longer have to live under a continuous low—lying cloud. A new power is in operation. The Spirit of life in Christ, like a strong wind, has magnificently cleared the air, freeing you from a fated lifetime of brutal tyranny at the hands of sin and death."

46. Joshua 24:15: "And if it seems evil to you to worship the Lord, choose for yourselves this day whom you will serve, whether the gods which your fathers served on the other side of the River, or the gods of the Amorites, in whose land you dwell; but as for me and my house, we will serve the Lord."

47. James 3:16: "For wherever there is jealousy (envy) and contention (rivalry and

selfish ambition) there will also be confu-
sion (unrest, disharmony, rebellion) and
all sorts of evil and vile practices."

48. Proverbs 4:20-22: "My son, attend to my
words; consent and submit to my sayings.
Let them not depart from your sight; keep
them in the center of your heart. For they
are life to those who find them, healing
and health to all their flesh."

49. Ephesians 1:19-21: "And (so that you can
know and understand) what is the immea-
surable and unlimited and surpassing
greatness of His power in and for us who
believe, as demonstrated in the working
of His mighty strength, which he exerted
in Christ when He raised Him from the
dead and seated Him at His (own) right
hand in the heavenly (places). Far above
all rule and authority and power and
dominion and every name that is named
(above every title that can be conferred),
not only in this world, but also in the age
and the world which are to come."

50. *1 John 4:17: "In this (union and communion with Him) love is brought to completion and attains perfection with us that we may have confidence for the Day of Judgment (with assurance and boldness to face Him), because as He is, so are we in this world."*

51. *Philippians 2:5: "Let this same attitude and purpose and (humble) mind be in you which was in Christ Jesus: (Let Him be your example in humility)."*

52. *Psalm 91:14: "Because he has set his love on Me, therefore I will deliver him; I will set him on high, because he knows and understands My name (has a personal knowledge of My mercy, love, and kindness—trusts and relies on Me, knowing I will never forsake him, no never)."*

53. *Hebrews 10:39: "But our way is not that of those who draw back to eternal misery (perdition) and are utterly destroyed, but we are of those who believe (who cleave to and trust in and rely on God through*

Jesus Christ, the Messiah) and by faith preserve the soul."

54. 1 John 3:2-3: "Beloved, we are (even here and) now God's children; it is not yet disclosed (made clear) what we shall be (hereafter), but we know that when He comes and is manifested, we shall (as God's children) resemble and be like Him just as He (really) is. And everyone who has this hope (resting) on Him cleanses and (purifies) himself just as He is pure (chaste, undefiled, guiltless)."

55. Hebrews 12:3: "Just think of Him who endured from sinners such grievous opposition and bitter hostility against Himself (reckon up and consider it all in comparison with our trials), so that you may not grow weary or exhausted, losing heart and relaxing and fainting in your minds."

56. Luke 12:31: "Only aim at and strive for and seek His kingdom, and all these things shall be supplied to you also."

57. Psalm 103:2-5 SEE NUMBER 39

58. John 14:12-14: *"I assure you, most solemnly I tell you, if anyone (steadfastly) believes in Me, he will himself be able to do the things that I do; and he will do even greater things than these, because I go to the Father. And I will do (I Myself will grant) whatever you ask in My Name (as presenting all that I AM) so that the Father may be glorified and extolled in (through) the Son. (Yes) I will grant (I Myself will do for you) whatever you shall ask in My Name (as presenting all that I AM)."*

59. Ephesians 2:10: *"For we are God's (own) handiwork (His workmanship), recreated in Christ Jesus, (born anew) that we may do those good works which God predestined (planned beforehand) for us (taking paths which He prepared ahead of time), that we should walk in them (living the good life which He prearranged and made ready for us to live)."*

60. Job 23:10: *"But He knows the way that I take (He has concern for it, appreciates,*

and pays attention to it). When He has tried me, I shall come forth as refined gold (pure and luminous)."

61. *Psalm 16:11: "You will show me the path of life; in Your presence is fullness of joy, at Your right hand there are pleasures forevermore."*

62. *Song of Solomon 2:4: "He brought me to the banqueting—house, and His banner over me was love (for love waved as a protecting and comforting banner over my head when I was near Him)."*

63. *Song of Solomon 7:10 (KJV): "I am my beloved's and His desire is toward me.*

64. *Psalm 119:170 (MSG): Give my request Your personal attention, rescue me on the terms of Your promise."*

65. *Romans 11:29: "For God's gifts and His call are irrevocable. (He never withdraws them when once they are given, and He does not change His mind about those to whom He gives His grace or to whom He sends His call)."*

66. *Romans 5:17: SEE NUMBER 10*

67. *Ephesians 1:17-18: "(For I always pray to) the God of our Lord Jesus Christ, the Father of glory, that He may grant you a spirit of wisdom and revelation (of insight into mysteries and secrets) in the (deep and intimate) knowledge of Him. By having the eyes of your heart flooded with light, so that you can know and under-stand the hope to which He has called you and how rich is His glorious inheri-tance in the saints (His set apart ones)."*

68. *Proverbs 4:7: "The beginning of Wisdom is: get Wisdom (skillful and godly Wisdom)! (for skillful and godly Wisdom is the prin-cipal thing.) And with all you have gotten, get understanding (discernment, compre-hension, and interpretation)."*

69. *Proverbs 4: 8-10: "Prize Wisdom highly and exalt her, and she will exalt and pro-mote you; she will bring you to honor when you embrace her. She shall give to your head a wreath of gracefulness; a crown*

of beauty and glory will she deliver to you. Hear, O my son, and receive my sayings, and the years of your life shall be many."

70. Matthew 10:36: "And a man's foes will be they of his own household."

71. Nehemiah 8:10b: "Be not grieved and depressed, for the joy of the Lord is your strength and stronghold."

72. Hebrews 12:3: SEE NUMBER 55

73. Romans 5:5: "Such hope never disappoints or deludes or shames us, for God's love has been poured out in our hearts through the Holy Spirit who has been given to us."

74. Psalm 42:11: "Why are you cast down, O my inner self? And why should you moan over me and be disquieted within me? Hope in God and wait expectantly for Him, for I shall yet praise Him, Who is the help of my countenance, and my God."

75. Isaiah 55:8-9: "For My thoughts are not your thoughts, neither are your ways My ways, says the Lord. For as the heavens

are higher than the earth, so are My ways higher than your ways and My thoughts than your thoughts."

76. 1 Samuel 16:7b: "For the Lord sees not as man sees; for man looks on the outward appearance, but the Lord looks on the heart."

77. Revelation. 7:9: "After this, I looked and a vast host appeared which no one could count, (gathered out) of every nation, from all tribes and peoples and languages. These stood before the throne and before The Lamb; they were attired in white robes, with palm branches in their hands."

78. Matthew 16:18: "And I tell you, you are Peter, (Greek, Petros—a large piece of rock), and on this rock (Greek, petra—a huge rock like Gibraltar) I will build my church and the gates of Hades (the powers of the infernal region) shall not overpower it (or be strong to its detriment or hold out against it)."

79. 2 Corinthians 3:1b: "But they, measuring themselves by themselves and comparing themselves among themselves, are not wise."

80. Revelation 15:3: "And they sang the song of Moses, the servant of God and the song of the Lamb, saying, Mighty and marvelous are your works, O Lord God the Omnipotent! Righteous (just) and true are Your ways, O Sovereign of the ages (King of the nations)!"

81. Matthew 15:3: "He replied to them, And why do you transgress and violate the commandment of God for the sake of the rules handed down to you by your forefathers (the elders)?"

82. Jeremiah 29:11: "For I know the thoughts and plans that I have for you, says the Lord, thoughts and plans for welfare and peace and not for evil, to give you hope in your final outcome."

83. Hebrews 10:34: "For you did sympathize and suffer along with those who

were imprisoned, and you bore cheer-
fully the plundering of your belongings
and the confiscation of your property, in
the knowledge and consciousness that
you yourselves had a better and lasting
possession."

84. Isaiah 55:8: SEE NUMBER 75

85. Romans 8:2-3: "For the law of the Spirit
of Life (which is) in Christ Jesus (the law
of our new being) has freed me from the
law of sin and of death. For God has done
what the law could not, (its power) being
weakened by the flesh (the entire nature
of man without the Holy Spirit) Sending
His own Son in the guise of sinful flesh
and as an offering for sin, (God con-
demned sin in the flesh (subdued, overcame, deprived it of its power over all who
accept that sacrifice)."

86. Acts 10:34: "And Peter opened his mouth
and said; Most certainly and thoroughly I
now perceive and understand that God

shows no partiality and is no respecter of persons."

87. Mark 8:36: "For what does it profit a man to gain the whole world, and forfeit his own life (in the eternal kingdom of God)?"

88. James 3:16 SEE NUMBER 47

89. Ephesians 6:12 "For we are not wrestling with flesh and blood (contending only with physical opponents), but against the powers, against the despotisms, against (the master spirits who are) the world rulers of this present darkness, against the forces of wickedness in the heavenly (supernatural) sphere."

90. Proverbs 3:6: "In all your ways know, recognize, and acknowledge Him, and He will direct and make straight and plain paths."

91. Isaiah 65:24: "And it shall be that before they call I will answer; and while they are yet speaking I will hear."

92. Philippians 3:12-14: "Not that I have now attained(this ideal), or have already been made perfect, but I press on to lay hold of

(grasp) and make my own, that for which Christ Jesus (the Messiah) has laid hold of me and made me His own. I do not consider, brethren, that I have captured and made it my own (yet); but one thing I do (it is my one aspiration): forgetting what lies behind and straining forward to what lies ahead, I press on toward the goal to win the (supreme and heavenly) prize to which God in Christ Jesus is calling us upward."

93. *John 15:26: "But when the Comforter (Counselor, Helper, Advocate, Intercessor, Strengthener, Standby) comes, Whom I will send to you from the Father, The Spirit of Truth Who comes (proceeds) from the Father He (Himself) will testify regarding Me."*

94. *Isaiah 60:1-3: "Arise (from the depression and prostration in which circumstances have kept you—rise to a new life)! Shine (be radiant with the glory of the Lord) for your light has come, and the glory of*

the Lord has risen upon you! For behold, darkness shall cover the earth, and dense darkness (all) peoples, but the Lord shall arise upon you (O Jerusalem), and His glory shall be seen on you. And nations shall come to your light, and kings to the brightness of your rising."

95. Romans 12:2: "Do not be conformed to this world (this age), fashioned after and adapted to its external, superficial customs), but be transformed (changed), so that you may prove (for yourselves) what is the good and acceptable and perfect will of God even the thing which is good and acceptable and perfect (in His sight for you)."

96. Psalm 33:1: SEE NUMBER 30

97. Isaiah 11:3-4: "And shall make Him of quick understanding, and His delight shall be in the reverential and obedient fear of the Lord. And He shall not judge by the sight of His eyes, neither decide by the hearing of His ears; But with righteousness and

justice shall He judge the poor and decide with fairness for the meek, the poor, and the downtrodden of the earth; and He shall smite the earth and the oppressor with the rod of His mouth, and with the breath of His lips He shall slay the wicked."

98. Matthew 25:40: *"And the King will reply to them, Truly I tell you, in so far as you did it for one of the least (in the estimation of men) of these My brethren, you did it for Me."*

99. 1st Chronicles 4:10a: *"Jabez cried to the God of Israel, saying, Oh, that You would bless me and enlarge my borders."*

100. Psalm 139:2: *"You know my down—sitting and my uprising; You understand my thoughts from afar off."*

101. Romans 8:7: *"That is because the mind of the flesh (with its carnal thoughts and purposes) is hostile to God, for it does not submit itself to God's Law; indeed it cannot."*

102. John 16:13: "But when He, the Spirit of Truth (the Truth-giving Spirit) comes, He will guide you into all the Truth (the whole Truth), For He will not speak His own message (on His own authority); but He will tell whatever He hears (from the Father; He will give the message that has been given to Him), and He will announce and declare to you the things that are to come (that will happen in the future)."

103. Proverbs 18:2: "A (self-confident) fool has no delight in understanding but only in revealing his personal opinions and himself."

104. Romans 5:15: "But God's free gift is not at all to be compared to the trespass (His grace is out of all proportion to the fall of man). For if many died through one man's falling away (his lapse, his offense), much more profusely did God's grace and the free gift (that comes) through the unde-served favor of the one Man Jesus Christ

abound and overflow to and for (the benefit) of many."

105. Proverbs 29:18a: "Where there is no vision (no redemptive revelation of God), the people perish."

106. Hebrews 12:26-29: "Then (at Mr. Sinai) His voice shook the earth, but now He has given a promise: Yet once more I will shake and make tremble not only the earth, but also the (starry) heavens. Now this expression, yet once more, indicates the final removal and transformation of all (that can be) shaken—that is, of that which has been created—in order that what cannot be shaken may remain and continue. Let us therefore receiving a kingdom that is firm and stable and cannot be shaken, offer to God pleasing service and acceptable worship with modesty and pious care and godly fear and awe."

107. John 14:26: "But the Comforter (Counselor, Helper, Intercessor, Advocate, Strengthener, Standby), The Holy spirit,

Whom the Father will send in My Name (in My place, to represent Me and act on My behalf), He will teach you all things. And He will cause you to recall (will remind you of, bring to your remembrance) everything I have told you."

108. *Job 3:25 (NLT): "What I always feared has happened to me. What I dreaded has come true."*

109. *Proverbs 6:4-5: MSG "Don't procrastinate—there's no time to lose. Run like a deer from the hunter, fly like a bird from the trapper!"*

110. *John 1 4-5: "In Him was Life, and the Life was the Light of men. And the Light shines on in the darkness, for the darkness has never overpowered it (put it out or absorbed it or appropriated it, and is unreceptive to it)."*

111. *John 8:44: "You are of your father, the devil, and it is your will to practice the lusts and gratify the desires (which are characteristic) of your father. He was a*

murderer from the beginning and does not stand in the truth, because there is no truth in him. When he speaks a falsehood; he speaks what is natural to him, for he is a liar (himself) and the father of lies and of all that is false."

112. *Deuteronomy 28:13: "And the Lord shall make you the head, and not the tail; and you shall be above only and you shall not be beneath, if you heed the commandments of the Lord your God which I command you this day and are watchful to do them."*

113. *Luke 10:19: "Behold I have given you authority and power to trample upon serpents and scorpions, and (physical and mental strength and ability) over all the power that the enemy (possesses); and nothing shall in any way harm you."*

114. *2 Corinthians 10:3-6 (MSG) "The world is unprincipled. It's dog eat dog out there! The world doesn't fight fair. But we don't live or fight our battles that way—never*

have and never will. The tools of our trade are not for marketing or manipulation, but they are for demolishing that entire massively corrupt culture. We use our God—tools for smashing warped philosophies, tearing down barriers erected against the truth of God, fitting every loose thought and emotion and impulse into the structure of life shaped by Christ. Our tools are ready at hand for cleaning the ground of every obstruction and building lives of obedience into maturity.

115. 1 Peter 4:8: "Above all things have intense and unfailing love for one another, for love covers a multitude of sins (forgives and disregards the offenses of others)."

116. Hebrews 13:8: "Jesus Christ (the Messiah) is (always) the same, yesterday, today, (yes) and forever (to the ages)."

117. Philippians 1:6: "And I am convinced and sure of this very thing, that He Who began a good work in you will continue until the

day of Jesus Christ *(right up to the time of His return)*, developing *(that good work)* and perfecting and bringing it to full completion in you.

118. Ephesians 3:12 *"In Whom, because of our faith in Him, we dare to have the boldness (courage and confidence) of free access (an unreserved approach to God with freedom and without fear.")*.

119. Psalm 100:4: *"Enter into His gates with thanksgiving and with a thank offering and into His courts with praise! Be thankful and say so to Him, bless and affectionately praise His name!"*

120. 3rd John 1:4 (MSG): *"Nothing could make Me happier than getting reports that My children continue diligently in the way of Truth."*

121. Proverbs 29:18: SEE NUMBER 105

122. Psalm 37:5: *"Commit your way unto the Lord (roll and repose each care of your load on Him); trust (lean on, rely on, and*

be confident) also in Him and He will bring
it to pass."

123. Philippians 1:6: SEE NUMBER 117

124. 1st Peter 5:4 "And (then) when the Chief
Shepherd is revealed, you will win the
conqueror's crown of glory."

125. Isaiah 30:21: "And your ears will hear a
word behind you, saying, This is the way;
walk in it, when you turn to the right hand
and when you turn to the left."

126. Romans 8:32 "He Who did not spare His
own Son also but gave Him up for us all,
will He not also with Him freely and gra-
ciously give us all (other) things?"

127. Hebrews 4:1 "Therefore, while the
promise of entering His rest still holds and
is offered (today), let us be afraid (to dis-
trust it), lest any or you should think he
has come too late and has come short of
(reaching) it."

128. John 17:21-22: "That they all may be one,
(just) as You, Father are in Me and I in You,
that they also may be one in Us, so that

the world may believe and be convinced that God has sent Me. I have given to them the glory and honor which You have given Me, that they may be one (even) as We are one."

CPSIA information can be obtained
at www.ICGtesting.com
Printed in the USA
FFOW05n2216160615

9 781498 4332